Aloha, Baby-sitters!

Aloha, Baby-sitters!

Ann M. Martin

AN
APPLE
PAPERBACK

SCHOLASTIC INC.
New York Toronto London Auckland Sydney

Cover art by Hodges Soileau

ISBN 0-590-22883-8

12 11 10 9 8 7 6 5 4 3 2   6 7 8 9/9 0 1/0

Printed in the U.S.A.   40

First Scholastic printing, July 1996

*The author gratefully acknowledges
Peter Lerangis
for his help in
preparing this manuscript.*

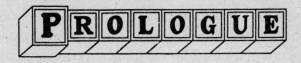

PROLOGUE

Friday

I, Jessica Ramsey, am going to Hawaii. How do I feel about that? I'll tell you in one word. YEEEaaaaaaaaaa!!!!!

Jessi

I'm dancing. I'm writing one sentence, then dancing around the room. *Tour jetés*. Good ones, better than I've ever done in ballet class.

I guess total ecstasy is good for coordination.

My aunt Cecelia is looking at me as if I've lost my mind. Well, maybe I have. This will be the farthest away from home I've ever traveled. And I'm going with all my best friends.

Well, almost all.

Mallory Pike can't go. When I think of that, I stop dancing.

Mal is my absolute number-one friend in the world. We're so alike, we can almost read each other's minds. We're both horse fanatics. We both love to read. We're both the oldest kids in our families. Our parents treat us alike, too — like babies — even though we're both eleven. Okay, we have differences. I love to dance, Mal loves to write and illustrate stories. She's Caucasian and I'm African-American. Still, we're like sisters.

Why can't Mal go to Hawaii? Timing, mostly. And money. You see, the trip was offered to us by our school, Stoneybrook Middle School, last month. We leave in three days, on the next-to-last Monday in July. Nothing like advance warning, huh? Luckily, I had no other plans for the month. But Mal does. She's helping her neighbor, Mrs. Stone, run a day camp on her farm.

Mal thought about finding someone to take her place. Mrs. Stone even said it would be okay. But when Mal mentioned the Hawaii trip to her parents, they said aloha. No way. Too expensive.

The Pikes just can't afford the trip. It takes a lot of money to support a family nearly the size of a baseball team. (Mallory has seven younger brothers and sisters.)

At first my parents didn't want me to go. But I told them it would be safe (fifty kids and six teacher chaperones are going). They finally agreed to pay for half the trip. I had to earn the other half. My best friends had the same half-and-half deal (yes, our parents did discuss this over the phone).

How did my friends and I raise the rest of the money? Well, we washed cars, mowed lawns, and held a special Fourth of July festival for kids. And we baby-sat like crazy, of course. We do a lot of that. We all belong to a group called the Baby-sitters Club, or BSC.

By the way, two other BSC members aren't going, either. Kristy Thomas is helping with Mrs. Stone's day camp, too (but *her* family is going to Hawaii in August, anyway). And Shannon Kilbourne is at summer camp.

Jessi

Today I decided I would prepare a special gift for Mallory. First I bought a beautiful scrapbook. Next I called all my BSC friends who are going on the trip and asked them to arrive at our regular club meeting twenty minutes early. Then, before Mallory showed up, I began writing in it.

By the time the meeting started, this is what the first page looked like:

Aloha!!!
A Hawaiian Travel Journal
Presented to Mallory Pike

We, the undersigned, being of sound mind and body, do hereby present to our friend Mallory Pike, who, due to circumstances beyond her control, could not join us

Jessi, puh-leeze! This isn't the U.S. Constitution!

I just want it to sound important, Stacey.

IF you want my OpiNioN, DEAR

Jessi

MALLORY IS JUST fine.

you gyes are turning this into a totle mess!!

(Please ignore the above comments from the peanut gallery.) Anyway,

Dear Mallory,

We wish you could have come with us on our trip to Hawaii. But since you couldn't, we decided to bring Hawaii to you. Well, at least Hawaii as we see it. We hope our journal will bring you some real solid aloha.

With Love From

Jessi
Stacey
Dawn

Claudia
MaryAnne
Abby

LOGAN

5

Jessi

Well, not exactly the neatest start.

That was okay. It would make Mallory laugh.

We all decided to write in spiral notebooks, then cut out our pages and paste them in the scrapbook.

I am determined to make this journal fantastic. I'm going to sightsee up a storm and write down every single detail. Not only that, I'm going to take along a camera and a tape recorder. For Mal's sake, I will dedicate myself to having the greatest trip ever.

Well, maybe not just for Mal's sake.

For mine, too, a little bit.

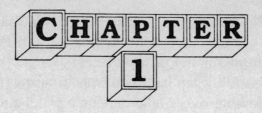

CHAPTER 1

Kristy

Friday

Okay, this is Kristy Thomas, reporting from home base. I don't know what has happened here. I am sitting in BSC headquarters, trying to start a meeting. We have lots to do. But the room has been invaded. All around me are strange, screaming creatures.

Mal, if this is what they're going to be like in Hawaii, I think we're better off here in Stoneybrook.

"Bluuuuuuue . . . bluuuuue Hawaaaaiiii . . ." Abby Stevenson sang as Logan Bruno strummed along on air ukelele.

"Yuck!" Claudia Kishi was draping pineapple rings over Mallomars on a plate, and the juice was dribbling onto her bedspread.

Stacey McGill held up a coconut, examining it as if it were some exotic moon stone. "How do you open this thing?"

My friends were sick with Hawaii fever.

To be honest, so was I. But I kept my sickness inside. In every Baby-sitters Club meeting, someone has to have two feet on the ground, even if everybody else is in the ozone layer.

Since I am club president, that someone is me.

I'm Kristy Thomas, by the way. I live in Stoneybrook, Connecticut, I'm thirteen years old, and I have medium-length brown hair. If you were a bug on Claudia's wall, you'd know exactly which girl was me — the short, loud one wearing old, casual clothes and a visor. My friends say I "dress down" (or worse), but I think that's ridiculous. I dress for comfort. And even though I'm just barely five feet tall, what I lack in height, I make up in energy and ingenuity.

Actually, I'm glad you weren't a bug on the

wall. I would have swatted you by now.

Just kidding.

Anyway, it was 5:27 on Friday. In three minutes, we would begin our last full meeting of the month. And in three days, on Monday, Mary Anne Spier, Abby Stevenson, Claudia Kishi, Jessi Ramsey, Stacey McGill, Dawn Schafer, and Logan Bruno were going to board a plane to Hawaii.

Why did *I* have Hawaii fever? Well, I was going to Hawaii, too, but not until August. It would have been nice to go with my best friends, but I'll settle for my family. They're cool.

They're large, too. Not large as in *fat*, but large as in *numerous*. That's because we're two families combined.

Family number one is the Thomases — my mom, my three brothers, and me. (Charlie is seventeen, Sam is fifteen, and David Michael is seven.) I suppose I should count my dad. I don't, usually. He left us soon after David Michael was born and hardly ever keeps in touch. (Frankly, I try not to think about him too much.)

Family number two is the Brewers. Watson Brewer, my stepdad, is a millionaire. When he fell in love with my mom, she was a single mother raising four kids. We lived in a small house across the street from Claudia and next door to Mary Anne. After Mom and Watson were married, we moved into Watson's mansion on the other side of town. I had never seen so many rooms in a house before. Plenty for everyone, including Watson's seven-year-old daughter and four-year-old son (Karen and Andrew) from a previous marriage. They live with us every other month, and with their mom in between.

Emily Michelle is the newest addition to our family. She's my two-year-old adopted sister, who was born in Vietnam. Objectively speaking, I do believe she's the most adorable child in Stoneybrook, if not the world. If you don't believe me, ask my grandmother, Nannie. She moved in with us shortly after Emily was adopted, and the two of them are super close.

Our other family members are Shannon (a puppy), Boo-Boo (a cat), and Crystal Light the Second and Goldfishie (goldfish). Emily Junior (a rat) and Bob (a hermit crab) belong to Karen and Andrew and travel back and forth with them.

Nowadays life is pretty easy for us. But back in the pre-Watson days, things could become hairy. Especially with Mom holding down a job and doing all the parenting. I was always trying to come up with ideas to make things easier. Even now, my friends call me the Idea

Machine. (They call me bossy and loud, too, but I won't go into that.)

My very best idea was the Baby-sitters Club.

I got the idea one day when Mom was having trouble finding a sitter for David Michael. I saw the yellow pages near the phone and I imagined a bold heading in it that said **BABY-SITTERS**. My first thought was, "Wouldn't it be great if finding a sitter were that simple?"

My second thought was, "Why not?" Okay, not a real company with a listing in the yellow pages, but a group of sitters that parents could call. All we needed were a phone number, a central headquarters, a good way to keep records, and some dedicated sitters.

We started with just Mary Anne, Claudia, and me. Nowadays we have seven members (ten, if you count our two associates and one honorary member). Claud has her own private phone line, so we use her room as headquarters. We meet from five-thirty to six o'clock, Monday, Wednesday, and Friday afternoons. Our clients call during those times to set up sitting jobs.

I, President Kristy, call the meetings to order and run them. But that's just part of my job. I also try to think about the Big Picture: new ideas for publicity, new ways to entertain our charges, and charity fund-raising events. Two of my favorite creations are Kid-Kits and the Krushers. No, that's not a rock group. Kid-Kits are boxes of toys, games, and other kid-related stuff we sometimes take with us on our jobs. The Krushers (*Kristy's* Krushers, to be exact) are a softball team. Technically it's not a BSC activity, but it's made up mainly of BSC charges who love to play softball. (I adore sports.)

I also invented the official BSC notebook. In it, we write about each of our jobs in detail, making sure to include kid news: who's been toilet-trained, who's lost an old fear or gained a new one, who's developed new likes and dislikes. We read it once a week, and it's a perfect way to keep each other up-to-date and prepared.

Claudia is our vice-president, mainly because she's the phone provider. But she does have one other major function: Club Appetite Spoiler.

Honestly, if Claudia's room ever caught fire, it would turn into one huge s'more. She has hidden away so many chocolates, candy bars, crackers, marshmallows, cookies, chips, and pretzels, she can't keep track of them all. Years from now, her granddaughter will discover a fuzzy, moldy Milky Way bar left over from Grandma Claud's BSC days.

Despite the high-fat, high-sugar, high-chocolate, low-good-stuff diet, Claudia isn't the least bit overweight. Her skin? Perfect (even though chocolate is supposed to give you zits). She doesn't exercise at all, either. I don't know how she does it.

Claudia is second-generation Japanese-American. That means her grandparents immigrated to the United States. In fact, her grandmother, Mimi, used to live with the Kishis. Mimi was a lot like Claudia — creative and funny and smart. When Mimi died, Claudia was devastated.

Unfortunately, the rest of the family is on a different planet from Claud. They're nice and all, but they're the kind of people who read only serious books, discuss science at the dinner table, and eat dull and healthy foods. They even forbid Claudia to read her favorite books, Nancy Drew mysteries, because they're too "frivolous." (Claud hides those in her room, too.) Janine, Claudia's older sister, has an IQ of two gazillion and takes college courses even though she's still in high school.

Claudia has enough trouble with middle-school courses. Her spelling and math are especially horrible. But put her in front of an easel and she's in her element. Claud's fantastic. She can paint, sculpt, draw, and make gorgeous jewelry. I guess you could call her an artistic dresser, too. She buys the ugliest junk at thrift shops and somehow turns it into cool outfits.

Stacey wears great clothes, too, but her theory of fashion is more cool-at-the-store, cool-on-the-body. Her style is Young Sophisticate. (At least that's the name of the section she shops in at Bellair's department store.) She spots all the hottest styles right away. (It's not stuff I would wear, but then Stacey calls my style Early Cro-Magnon.)

As BSC treasurer, Stacey collects our weekly dues and handles the club finances. That means paying Claudia for her phone bill; paying my brother Charlie, who chauffeurs Abby and me to and from meetings; buying supplies for Kid-Kits; and saving money for our special events.

Stacey has long, golden-blonde hair. She was born and raised on the streets of New York City (well, actually, in an apartment). She moved to Stoneybrook when her dad's company relocated to Connecticut. We snapped her up into the BSC. Then — *whoosh!* — another relocation, back to NYC. We thought we'd lost her for good. But Mr. and Mrs. McGill, who hadn't been getting along too well, finally divorced, and Stacey ended up moving to Stoneybrook again, this time with just her mom.

Stacey has a boyfriend named Robert Brewster, who is also going on the Hawaii trip. He's tall and cute and athletic. He used to play on the SMS basketball team, but he quit, partly in protest over the cruel way the school cheerleaders treated Stacey when she tried out for the squad. (*That's* dedication.) He's also very sensitive to Stacey's special health needs. You see, she has diabetes. Her body doesn't produce enough insulin, a hormone that regulates blood sugar. If Stacey eats too much sugar, she could go into a coma. But she can lead a perfectly normal life as long as she eats meals on a rigid schedule, avoids sweets, and injects herself with artificial insulin every day. Stacey insists that the last part's not gross at all.

It's a good thing she never does it in front of Mary Anne, though. Mary Anne would pass out. She is the most sensitive person I've ever met. Also the shyest and kindest and sweetest. And my all-time best friend. (I know what's on your mind — "opposites attract" — and you're not the first to think of it.) Mary Anne tends to cry a lot. Her boyfriend, Logan, says they'll need a mop for the tarmac when we're saying good-bye at the airport.

Mary Anne's the club secretary. When a call comes in, we turn to her. She keeps the BSC record book, which has a calendar of our jobs. In her small, neat handwriting, she records all of our conflicts: doctor appointments, lessons, family trips, and extracurricular activities. She lets us know who's available for each job request, then helps assign the job, trying to divide the work equally. In the back of the book, she keeps a list of all our clients' names and addresses, the rates they pay, and information about their kids.

Mary Anne inherits her quiet, neat nature from her dad. Maybe the sweetness comes from her mom, but we'll never know. Mrs. Spier died when Mary Anne was a baby, and Mary Anne's dad raised her alone. He kind of went overboard with rules, I guess because he felt he had to be Mr. Superparent. Mary Anne is pretty and petite, with dark brown hair and a nice figure, but her dad made her dress like a little girl right up through seventh grade.

Eventually he did ease up, thank goodness. And his life (and Mary Anne's) took a huge turn for the better. First Dawn Schafer moved to Stoneybrook from California with her younger brother and their divorced mom. Next, Dawn and Mary Anne became friends. Then they discovered that their parents had been high school sweethearts. Before you knew it, Dawn was a BSC member, the two old folks were walking down the aisle, Mary Anne had a great mom and stepsister, and they all moved into Mrs. Schafer's old farmhouse. (Dawn's brother, Jeff, hated Stoneybrook from the get-go and moved back in with his dad long before the wedding.)

These days, Dawn is our honorary member. She's visiting us for the summer. She used to be a regular member, until she moved back to California to live with her dad, her brother, and her stepmother.

Dawn is also the world's foremost All-natural Baby-sitter. She won't touch red meat. She writes letters to congresspeople against rain forest destruction. If a study showed that grass was nutritious, Dawn would graze for her supper.

She's really opinionated and independent, which I admire. But she's also fun to be around and always cheerful. She has the looooongest hair, down past her waist, which is the absolute lightest shade of blonde before pure white.

I find it pretty weird that Dawn came all the way to Connecticut to visit and now she's flying off to Hawaii — but hey, life is for living, right?

After Dawn returned to California, we went without an official replacement for awhile. Our two junior officers, Jessi Ramsey and Mallory Pike, handled a lot of extra daytime jobs (they're eleven, and their parents don't allow them to baby-sit at night unless it's for their own siblings). Our two associates worked overtime, too. They're kind of our reserve forces. Normally they're not required to attend meetings or pay dues — which is a good thing, because both of them are involved in lots of after-school activities. One of them, Shannon Kilbourne, lives in my neighborhood and goes to a private school called Stoneybrook Day School. She has thick, curly blonde hair and high cheekbones. The other is Logan Bruno, Mary Anne's boyfriend. Yes, he's a boy (and yes, I think he spends too much time with Mary Anne), but I admit he's a great sitter. He has wavy hair, a dimply smile, and a trace of a southern accent (he comes from Louisville, Kentucky).

Anyway, even with Logan's and Shannon's help, we were going crazy with an overload of job requests. We needed help, big-time.

Right around then, Abby and Anna Stevenson—thirteen-year-old twins who love kids —moved into a house on my block. I mean, is that luck or what? I got to know them, introduced them to my friends, and our problem was solved! Abby became our new alternate officer. We offered Anna membership, too, but she turned it down. She's super-serious about her violin playing and practices for hours every day. (Me? I'd rather listen to screaming kids than a squeaky fiddle.)

Abby and Anna are identical twins, but you'd have no trouble telling them apart. Abby's about as musical as a tree stump. She's very athletic and has a crazy sense of humor. Her hair is a thick, wild volcano of dark brown curls. Because of her asthma, she carries around an inhaler all the time, and she's allergic to just about anything you can think of. Anna's nonallergic and nonasthmatic, she doesn't like sports at all, and her hair is cut in a short, pageboy style.

Actually, I take back what I said about Abby being nonmusical. At Friday's meeting, she was being way *too* musical.

"Da-da-da-da-daaaaaa-daaaaa!" Now she was singing the theme to *Hawaii Five-O*, pretending to row Claudia's bed.

Fortunately, the clock clicked to 5:30. "This meeting will come to order!" I announced.

"EEEEE!" Abby screeched, lurching backward.

"What was that?" asked Claudia.

"The brakes," Abby replied.

"Canoes don't have brakes," Stacey said.

"Ahem. I have some new business." I pulled a T-shirt out of a plastic bag I'd brought. "I had these specially made for all of us at the Washington Mall."

I held up the shirt and showed off the print on the front and back:

THE BABY-SITTERS CLUB
Call KL5-3231

"Cool," Stacey said.

"We're supposed to wear them in Hawaii?" Claudia asked.

"A new fashion statement on the beaches of Waikiki," Abby remarked.

"It's just so you can *remember who you are*," I said in my best Mufasa imitation.

I handed them out, and everyone put one on.

"Hey, I have some new business." Claudia reached into her night-table drawer and pulled out a sheet of paper. "An official reading of the itinerary. Ahem. We land on . . . um, Oahu island." Claudia pronounced the name *Oh-hoo.*

"It's *Oh-AH-hoo*," Jessi corrected her.

"Right," Claudia said. "Then five glorious days in Honolulu, with trips to Waikiki Beach, Pearl Harbor, and Manoa Valley. Then the trip splits. One small group, including Stacey, will fly to the island of, um . . ."

"Maui," Stacey said, pronouncing it *MOW-ee*, with an *ow* as in *pow*.

"There, they will explore a park with a totally unpronounceable name, but I'm not going there so I won't even try. The rest of us will spend four days in Windward . . . Ohio,

20

or however you say it, followed by a day-long trip to the North Shore — "

"Where the best surfers are," Dawn informed us.

"Then back to Honolulu and a flight home!" Claudia finished.

"Very cool," Abby said.

"We'll miss you guys a lot," Mallory spoke up.

"Us, too," Stacey replied.

"I wish you were coming," Jessi said softly.

She and Mal threw their arms around each other, sniffling away.

Mary Anne gave me a hangdog look. Her eyes were starting to water, too.

"Hey, we'll be seeing each other at the airport," I said.

But the Spier Waterworks were flowing, so I gave Mary Anne a hug. I'm much less emotional about things like this. I only cry at really serious stuff.

I hope Mary Anne didn't feel the tears drip onto the back of her new BSC T-shirt.

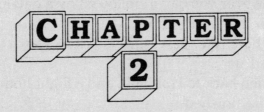

Abby

Monday

Dogs.
Dust.
Kitty litter.
Pollen.
Tomatoes.
Shellfish.
Milk.
Cheese.
Now I have one
more allergy to
add to my list.
Early mornings...

Take my advice. Do not ever, *ever* wake up at four o'clock in the morning unless you absolutely have to. It may not be the world's most horrible experience, but it's close.

I guess my alarm went off. I wouldn't know. I was in the Outer Limits of Sleep.

I was dreaming about Don Ho. Remember him? He's the singer in those TV reruns of *Hawaii Five-O*. I'd been watching that, plus *Magnum P.I.*, on the nighttime oldies channel. I kind of prefer Tom Selleck to Don Ho, but I was having a chat with old Don in my dream.

And his voice started sounding a lot like my mom's.

"Good morning!" chirped Don.

Morning? It was the middle of the night. I grumbled and turned over.

"Time to wake up!"

My eyes sprang open.

Don Ho was my mom.

She'd turned on a lamp in my room, but it was pitch-black outside.

"It's tibe?" I asked.

Oh, great. My allergies were checking in.

Mom smiled and nodded. "Can I fix you breakfast?"

"Nahh, I'll do it."

"Okay, see you downstairs."

I creaked upward. My nose was stuffed. My

eyes were swollen. I felt as if I'd just been through a Cuisinart. My clock said 4:01. I've gone to bed that late before. This was definitely not a wake-up time. I came *this* close to plopping back down to my favorite position.

Then I thought about Don. And that made me think about Hawaii. Where, in a few short hours, I would be.

Zzzzoom. I was up, dressed, and downstairs.

My sister, Anna, was sitting with Mom at the breakfast table, eating a bowl of cereal. Anna looked soggier than her Wheat Chex. "Bordig!" I said. "What are you doig up?"

"I just wanted to see you off," Anna replied. (Don't I have a sweet sister?)

"Thagks!" I gave her a hug and headed for the cupboard.

As I poured myself some cereal, Mom began the questioning:

"Did you pack your inhalers?" she asked.

"Yes, Bob," I replied. "Last dight."

"Enough decongestant for ten days?"

"Yup. But if I rud out, I thigk they have stores in Hawaii."

"A bathing suit?"

"Yes, Bob."

"Beach towels?"

"Yes, Bob."

Somehow I managed to shovel in some Chex during the grilling.

Anna and I chatted for awhile afterward. She reminded me to send postcards and take pictures. I brought out travel brochures and showed her where we were going, for the ten thousandth time. Mom hovered over us, frowning. She kept steering the conversation around to sun poisoning, tidal waves, and diarrhea, but mostly we ignored her.

When breakfast was over, I ran upstairs to finish packing. Okay, maybe not finish. Continue.

Well, I guess *start* would be the best word.

Cut Arnold Schwarzenegger out of the movie poster for *Terminator*. Replace him with a picture of me, cross out the title, and call it *Procrastinator*.

It's a documentary of my life.

I opened my suitcase. I went to my dresser and removed the contents of Drawer Number One, and shoved it into the suitcase. All underwear and bathing suits. About three-quarters of Drawer Number Two (summer shirts) made it, and the same with Drawer Number Three (shorts, skirts). Then I human-vacuumed the bottom of my closet for shoes and dumped them in, too.

Don't worry. I eyeballed all of it for design coordination. Everything matched, more or less.

Next stop, the bathroom. I picked up my

Abby

brush and performed my morning wrestling match with my hair. Then I washed up, brushed my teeth, and threw all of the appropriate stuff into my travel kit.

I ran back to my room and quickly went through Abby's Five Phases of Packing: Shock, Denial, Anger, Bargaining, and Mourning. Shock that the suitcase won't close, denial that I have too much stuff, anger at the fact that I didn't pack earlier, bargaining with the objects to make room for one another, and mourning for the clothes I must leave behind.

"Are you ready yet?" my mom called from downstairs.

I glanced at the clock. Four-forty-five. The buses were supposed to leave from SMS at five o'clock sharp.

"Albost!" I lied.

I did a fast check of the room. Quickly I stuffed a book and a magazine into the gaps of the suitcase and closed it.

Dragging the zipper across it was a feat of strength only a true Procrastinator could accomplish. Finally, with the suitcase closed, I tried to lift it.

Ugh. Not in this lifetime.

"Help!" I called out.

You should have seen Anna and me trying to maneuver the beast down the stairs. We were laughing so hard I thought we'd keel over. I don't know how we managed to take it out of the house and lift it into the back of Mom's minivan.

Mom drove us to SMS. There, in small pools of streetlamp light, kids and parents were hugging and talking in hushed voices. Dim light shone from the buses' cargo holds, which were already crowded with luggage.

The neighborhood houses were dark and still. Crickets still chirped, and a cool breeze made goose bumps rise on my arms.

"Eerie, huh?" Anna remarked.

We parked at the end of the block, behind a line of cars. Luckily, Stacey and Robert spotted us and helped drag the beast to the bus.

"Now," Mom said as I hugged her good-bye, "are you sure you have — "

"Yes, Bob!" Anna and I said together. (Anna does an expert imitation of my allergy-speak.)

Mary Anne, Logan, and Dawn were already on the bus, yammering away. For some reason, Logan was not sitting next to Mary Anne, so I did. Stacey and Robert slid into the seats across the aisle from us.

Jessi bounced onto the bus a few minutes later. You should have seen her leaping down the aisle.

Claudia arrived last (surprise, surprise). We peered through the window as her family tried to load two enormous suitcases into the jammed cargo hold. It was like watching a pair of tardy hippos crowding onto Noah's ark.

Claud and Jessi sat behind Stacey and Robert. We all started talking at once.

We didn't stop until we reached the New York State border. The sun was up. That somehow reminded us of how tired we should be, and we all fell asleep.

We awoke to the voice of Mr. Kingbridge, the SMS assistant principal. "Rise and shine, troops, we're here!"

"Hawaii?" Jessi exclaimed groggily.

When I opened my eyes, I half-expected to see palm trees.

"I don't think so," Claudia said. "This is a tour bus, not the Magic School Bus."

We were in front of the airline terminal at John F. Kennedy International Airport in New York City. As the bus doors opened, we scrambled out onto the sidewalk.

I could not believe the number of people traveling at 6:45 A.M. We had to wait in a long line at the check-in counter.

But when we were done, we still had an hour left, so we had breakfast. Again.

I was just finishing up a Danish when a voice blared over a loudspeaker: "Now boarding flight two-fourteen to Los Angeles Airport, at gate five."

I took a leisurely sip of orange juice.

Mrs. Hall, an English teacher who was sitting at our table, stood up. "That's us!"

I nearly choked. "Huh?" I said. "Los Angeles? Did they change the trip on us?"

Dawn rolled her eyes. "We lay over there, then we change planes to Hawaii."

Duh.

I pulled some money out of my pocket, but Mrs. Hall said, "Put it back. Mr. Kingbridge is paying."

We all gave him a "Two-four-six-eight-who-do-we-appreciate" cheer. He blushed like crazy.

Then we left the coffee shop and barged through the airport, parting the crowds of rushing people. As we lined up to go through the metal detector, Alan Gray, the Head Goon of the eighth grade, cut in front of us.

"He'll never make it," Claudia muttered. "His pinhead will set off the alarm."

Guess what? He did set it off! It was just because of something in his pocket, but we burst into giggles anyway.

We giggled all the way onto the plane. When the flight attendant demonstrated the emergency stuff, it was as if we were at a comedy show. We just could not stop. I don't know why.

We settled down somewhere over Pennsylvania, when the flight attendants brought us our third breakfast. I couldn't believe how hungry I was. I actually ate it.

All the SMS kids and chaperones were basically in the same area of the plane. I had a window seat, next to Claudia. (Mary Anne, to my surprise, still was not sitting next to Logan.) But once the seat-belt sign was off, no one stayed put. The cabin became one big party. I switched seats with Dawn to talk to Jessi. Mary Anne switched seats with Jessi to talk to me. Kids I barely knew were strolling up and down the aisle, being friendlier than they ever had been in school.

Especially some blonde girl I didn't know, who was flirting with Robert Brewster. I glanced over at Stacey, but she was sitting with Jessi, facing away from Robert. I decided not to worry about it. Everyone was feeling kind of open and excited.

Well, except Alan Gray, who was just feeling dorky. He was holding up a rubbery omelette and pretending it was alive.

When the flight attendant announced that it was in-flight movie time, we scrambled back to our seats.

The movie? Fine. The rest of the flight? Fast. I was in the middle of a long conversation with Claud when a voice announced, "We are now beginning our descent to the Los Angeles area. . . ."

Abby

I was shocked. The flight sure hadn't seemed five hours long.

How was L.A.? Well, I did not see one movie star in the airport, but I did see someone with a pet iguana. We were there long enough to (1) hear a lecture on behavior from Mr. Kingbridge and (2) set our watches back three hours. (That meant we'd left New York at eight o'clock and were in L.A. at ten o'clock. Not bad, huh? Sometimes it takes me that long just to get out of bed.)

You know what was the nicest part of the layover? Dawn's brother, stepmother, and father were there to meet her. She was sooooo surprised.

Before we knew it, we were trudging onto another plane. Once again, we sat together. Once again, we made noise and disturbed our fellow passengers. But this flight had a boring movie, and the "lunch" almost made me lose my lunch.

I don't know about you, but I've always pictured California and Hawaii in about the same area. Boy, was I wrong. We were in the air five more hours. I had another snooze.

All that travel time was worth it, though. As our plane came down over the island of Oahu, I shrieked. You could see miles and miles of beaches and gorgeous green mountains. It looked like paradise.

And I was ready for the time of my life.

CHAPTER 3

Mary Anne

Monday

We're here!
I never, never want
to leave. Ever. This is
the most beautiful
place on earth. The
air is warm but
breezy. The people are
relaxed. Beaches stretch
out on one side, mountains
on the other.
And we've barely
left the airport!
I can't wait to see
Honolulu and Waikiki.
Neither can anyone else.
We're all screaming
like little kids.

MaryAnne

*Even Logan. He's
recovered from his
big shock at the
Honolulu airport....*

Sorry about my handwriting. I wrote that on the bus from Honolulu International Airport, so it was a little shaky.

Poor Logan. He seemed really excited as we left the plane, but his face kind of sagged inside the terminal. I figured he was tired. We all were. We'd been awake for fifteen hours and traveling for eleven of them. Our bodies were telling us it was seven at night, but the airport clocks all said two o'clock in the afternoon.

On the way to the baggage claim area, I was gabbing away with my BSC friends. Logan was looking around, not meeting my eyes.

Was he mad at me?

I was feeling nervous. Logan's my boyfriend, and we'd had a long talk before we left. You see, our friends had been giving us grief lately. They'd complained that Logan and I were spending too much time together. Part of me thought they should mind their own business. But part of me thought they were right. It's not fair to neglect your best friends.

So Logan and I decided on an experiment. We'd spend our vacation TBI — together but independent. Each of us would mainly hang out with our own friends. We wouldn't make it a big deal. We wouldn't *avoid* each other. We'd just feel free to be apart.

I thought things had been going well so far. We'd sat apart on the bus from Stoneybrook to New York and on both plane rides. That hadn't been too bad. We'd managed to chat a little.

But right now Logan did not look happy. Something was wrong. Was it something I said? Did I give off the wrong signal? Was TBI working too well?

"Logan," I said softly, "is everything okay?"

He glanced at me quickly, then looked away. "Well, I thought . . . nahhh, never mind."

Great. Here we were in the world's most beautiful spot, and Logan wanted to break up. Just my luck.

I wanted to cry. "Go ahead," I said. "Ask."

"Well . . . aren't we all supposed to get *leis* when we land? You know, like they did on *The Brady Bunch*?"

"*Leis?*"

Logan blushed. "I know, I know. Dumb question. It's just a TV show, right?"

"Right." I smiled and nodded.

Boy, did I feel stupid for worrying.

"Okay, kids, listen up," Mr. Kingbridge called out as we all gathered near the luggage conveyor belt. "For the purpose of traveling from here to the hotel in an orderly way, I will assign ten of you to each teacher. You will not have to stay in these groups throughout the trip. Each morning at breakfast we will post a few different itineraries, and you must sign up for one each day . . ."

"Can I book the beach group in advance?" Abby murmured to me.

Mr. Kingbridge went on for awhile about safety precautions — never leaving your camera or your money unattended on a beach blanket, making sure to lock up valuables in the hotel safe, stuff like that — then assigned all-boy and all-girl groups. I was in the same one as Abby, Stacey, Claudia, Dawn, and Jessi.

"How old-fashioned," Claudia remarked. "Separating the boys and girls."

Stacey shrugged. "So? That's okay with me."

That was not what I'd expect her to say. For so long, it's been impossible to tear Stacey and Robert apart. She was ecstatic when Robert's parents had agreed to let him go on the trip.

But now Robert was at the other end of the

conveyor belt with his friends and a girl named Sue Archer.

Hmmm. Were Stacey and Robert having their own TBI?

As Stacey leaned toward the belt to pick up her luggage, I glanced at Claudia. She raised one eyebrow. She'd noticed, too.

I have to confess something. On our flight from L.A. to Honolulu, Claudia had spotted Stacey and Robert arguing in the little area near the bathrooms. Claud figured Stacey was jealous of Robert's friends.

Maybe Sue had something to do with this, too.

"Oops, SOS!" Abby called out. "Come on, guys!"

Poor Stacey was valiantly trying to pull two humongous suitcases and a backpack off the belt. Abby, Claudia, and I ran to help her.

Next, Claudia's two Wonder Cases came rolling toward us. Honestly, they were so heavy I don't know why the belt didn't just grind to a halt.

Stacey, Abby, and Jessi wrestled one of them to the ground. If I hadn't rushed to help Claudia with the other, she might have been pulled onto the belt herself.

We were very lucky that Mr. De Young was assigned to our group. He's the boys' gym teacher, and he's built a little like Jean-Claude Van Damme. With his help, we managed to move all our luggage out of the terminal and onto a minibus emblazoned with the name of our hotel, the Honolulu Surf.

As we rolled away from the airport, I began to see why everyone loves Hawaii.

Even from the freeway, it looked spectacular. I'd seen palm trees before, in L.A., when I visited Dawn. But there, they looked like giant Q-Tips reaching up to swab the gray, polluted air. Here, they seemed tall and proud.

The air was clear. The grass was lush and green. Huge, ridged mountains rose on one side of us. On the other, a turquoise bay stretched out toward the ocean.

"Aloha and welcome to Hawaii," our bus driver announced over the speakers. "To your left is the Ko'olau Mountain Range, which is actually the rim of an extinct volcano. The Hawaiian Islands are formed entirely of volcanic lava. The smooth kind is called *pahoehoe*. The other kind is called *a'a*, and you'll discover why if you step on it . . . ."

The driver was pretty corny, but none of us minded. We were too busy gaping.

About fifteen minutes later we pulled up in front of our hotel. It was a squat, rectangular, four-story, glass-and-steel building in the middle of town.

"This is it?" Stacey asked.

Mr. De Young smiled. "You were expecting the Plaza?"

"No, but this is the Honolulu *Surf*," Stacey explained. "Where's the surf?"

Claudia shrugged. "You can make one in the tub."

"Hang ten on the bathmat," Abby said.

"Catch a shredder through your Mr. Bubble," Dawn added.

"Gnarly, dudes," Jessi remarked.

Mr. De Young must have thought we were out of our minds.

The minivan doors opened, and we all filed out. It was like walking into a perfume factory. Vibrant, thick-petaled flowers ringed the hotel.

Jessi was doing pirouettes in the parking lot.

"What's that thing?" Abby asked.

She was looking at a tree with gnarled bark and drooping branches. One of the branches had drooped all the way to the ground — and there it had taken root!

"A banyan tree," Dawn explained. "They don't have them in the Northeast."

"Thank you, Ms. Natural," Logan piped up out of nowhere. "Will you be eating the leaves raw or steamed for dinner tonight?"

Dawn chased Logan around the van.

For fifty jet-lagged, weary travelers, we sure made a lot of noise. Fortunately, the hotel had a few big, sturdy dollies to carry in our suitcases, plus a crew of big, sturdy staff members to push them.

As part of our package deal, we were to stay three to a room, on twin beds and a fold-out couch. Claudia, Dawn, and I were given Room 323. Stacey, Jessi, and Abby were assigned to another floor, but good old Abby fixed that. She found out who was in the room next to us and swapped keys.

After all the rooms had been assigned, Mr. Kingbridge announced, "Our main activities begin tomorrow. Today's pretty casual. Settle in your rooms and meet back here in half an hour if you're interested in a little stroll before dinner."

"YEEEAAAAAA!"

A bellhop helped us up to our room. (He almost had a heart attack when he lifted Claudia's suitcases.) Then he stood in the doorway with a pleasant smile.

"Thanks a lot," Claudia said. "Really."

He nodded and kept smiling, but he didn't move.

Claudia nodded, too. "Well . . . 'bye!" She stuck out her hand awkwardly, as if to shake his.

"Oops," Abby muttered. She fumbled around in her pocket, pulled out a few dollar bills, and handed them to the bellhop. He smiled even wider, thanked her, and left.

"You have to pay them to leave?" Claudia asked.

"It's called a tip, Claudia," Abby said.

"Oh."

"Should we unpack?" I asked.

Abby looked at Claudia's luggage. "You want to be here until midnight? Let's do it later. Maybe we can order an extra chest of drawers from room service."

We quickly washed up. Then we pulled fresh clothes from our suitcases, changed, and went back downstairs.

Everyone gathered in the hotel banquet room, then set off in chaperone-led groups. (I almost went with Logan's group, until I remembered TBI.)

After a few minutes, I started pooping out. But I do remember some things about our walk. Honolulu is super clean, for one thing. A lot of Hawaiians wear flip-flops in the city — and they really do wear gaudy Hawaiian shirts. Flowers are everywhere. And the open-air markets sell everything from octopus to exotic fruits. I bought a "hand" of tiny bananas and a star-shaped fruit called carambola.

Mary Anne

Dawn bought a breadfruit, which looks like an old grapefruit with acne.

I loved being around real Hawaiians. I couldn't wait to meet some and find out more about their culture.

When we returned to the hotel, we had an early dinner. I was so drowsy, I could barely focus on the menu.

Jessi was frowning at hers. "What's *mahi-mahi*?" she asked a waiter.

"Dolphin," he replied.

I thought Dawn would spit out the guava juice she was drinking. "But you can't — "

"A dolphin *fish*," the waiter said with a sly wink. "It's different from the mammal."

"What's *poi* bread?" Claudia asked.

"The opposite of girl bread," Abby replied.

"You don't know *poi*?" the waiter asked. "To Hawaiians, it's like rice. It's made from a root vegetable, *taro*. Never heard of it? I'll bring you some."

Well, I tried the *mahimahi* and the *poi* bread, and they were great. I washed it all down with papaya-mango juice, and I felt like a real Hawaiian.

We all trudged to our rooms at six-thirty. I plopped right into bed. The last thing I saw before my eyes closed was Claudia Kishi.

Unpacking.

CHAPTER 4

Jessi

Tuesday.

Hi Mallory. I'm writing you from Room 32 in the Honolulu Surf Hotel. It's 5:58 A.M. and I'm wide awake. Where you are, it's two minutes before eleven. Would you believe that Abby and Stacey are still asleep?

Anyway, I told you I'd bring Hawaii to you, so here it is. I will be your eyes, ears, nose, mouth, and hands. After you read this, see

my photos, and
hear my tape,
you'll think you
were here!
Okay. First, ears.
Right now, Abby
is snoring. I AM NOT.
Eyes. The sun is
rising outside the
window, just
behind the Ko'olau
Mountains. (See
photo.) Seagulls are
flying by, and a
black bird with
weird yellow eyes.
(Mrs. Gonzalez says
they're mynah birds.)
Nose. When I
woke up, I could
smell salt air
through the open
window. Also
coconuts and poi
bread baking in the
hotel kitchen. Do
you know what
poi is? . . .

"**W**hoa, leave some room for the rest of us!"

Stacey's voice gave me a start. I hadn't even realized she was awake.

"I haven't written *that* much," I said. "Yet."

"Zzzzzzzzzzzz," remarked Abby.

"Ahhh," Stacey said. "The call of the ancient Hawaiian sinus bird."

"That's funny," I said, scribbling away. "Mal will like that."

Stacey shuffled off to the bathroom.

A few minutes later I could see Abby's arm reaching out. Her eyes were still shut, but she knew just where to find the tissue box.

She held a tissue to her nose and honked.

"I dote doe what it is," she murmured. "Baybe I'b allergic to palb trees."

"Morning," Stacey said, emerging from the bathroom.

"Bordig, Stacey and Jessi," Abby replied as she gathered up a handful of rattling bottles. "Bordig, decodgestadt. Bordig, adtihistabine. Bordig, idhalers."

She walked to the bathroom, calling over her shoulder, "Pardod be while I try to becub a hubad."

I quickly wrote in Mal's journal:

*Abby's up. Also
stuffed up. For a
minute I thought
she said she
wanted to become
a Cuban. . . .*

When Abby returned, I washed up and dressed in record time. Breakfast was due to begin at six-thirty, and I was starving.

Before we left, I shut the spiral notebook and stuck it in my backpack. Then I tossed in my camera. I wanted both of them with me at all times.

Guess who was sitting on the carpet just outside the banquet room? Claudia, Dawn, Mary Anne, and about a dozen other SMS kids. (Everyone else in the hotel must have still been sleeping.)

"Hi!" we all called out.

Click. I took a photo of the gathering.

"Puh-leeze," Claudia protested. "Not before breakfast. I don't photograph well when I'm hungry."

"You just ate a whole bag of Doritos upstairs," Dawn said.

"Not true!" Claudia shot back. "I gave you three of them."

Soon the doors opened. Claudia was the first in line. The rest of us BSC members were close behind.

Click. I thought Mal would want to see a typical hotel breakfast. The buffet included a few funky-looking dishes, but fortunately everything was labeled. (Mary Anne and Dawn tried some of the *taro* pudding, but I stuck with scrambled eggs and sausage.)

After breakfast we split into groups. The majority wanted to go to the beach — including Abby, Stacey, Dawn, Robert, and Logan. Claudia, Mary Anne, and I all decided to sign up for a guided walking tour of Honolulu.

Mrs. Hall led us a few blocks away from the hotel to a fancy building with a lot of columns. In front of it was a statue of a stern-looking guy wearing a thick gold robe and an ugly hat, with a spear in one hand and his other hand raised palm up as if he'd just pitched a softball.

Waiting by the statue was our tour guide, a roly-poly, silver-haired man wearing flip-flops and a loud patterned shirt.

Click. The statue.

Click. The guide.

Click. The building (with Claudia in front, sticking out her tongue).

"Aloha and welcome," the guide said. "I am Mr. Yap and in case you're wondering about this statue, well, he's an Italian model."

I opened my spiral notebook and started writing:

Jessi

Italian model . . .

Mr. Yap grinned. "Actually, he's supposed to represent Kamehameha the Great, a warrior king who took Hawaii into the nineteenth century in a blaze of glory, only to see it start to fall apart. . . ."

Camahamahama or something . . .

Mr. Yap went on to talk about the late-1700s arrival in Hawaii of an English sea captain, James Cook. The Hawaiians thought he was a god. It took them awhile to realize he wasn't, and boy, were they angry. By that time, the Europeans had brought diseases and strange customs to the islands. The Hawaiians ended up killing Cook.

"Later, in the nineteenth century, the cultures really collided," Mr. Yap continued. "Missionaries were shocked by the Hawaiians' scanty clothing, and they invented the *muumuu* for the native women to wear. Looking into the houses of the missionaries, the Hawaiians were further shocked to see women cooking, and men sharing food at the same table as women. The Hawaiian system of behavior, *kapu*, allowed none of those things. Eventually, the Europeans forced *kapu* to die off and instituted their own customs."

What a familiar story this was.

Treatment of Hawaiians similar to horrible treatment of Africans and Native Americans around the same time in history . . . .

My head was buried in the notebook as Mr. Yap took us across the street and into a park. He showed us the only royal palace in the United States, 'Iolani Palace. (What did it look like? I don't remember. I was so busy writing, I only looked up to take a quick snapshot, and then I had to run to catch up with everybody.)

As we walked through the Hawaii capitol district, we saw the State Capitol, which has columns made to look like palms and rooms in the shape of volcanoes. (I took lots of cool pictures there.) We went to the Mission Houses Museum, a small complex of restored houses actually built by the missionaries, including a teeny bedroom where an entire family of seven slept.

I had to change rolls of film on our way to the Hawaii Maritime Center. There I scribbled like crazy:

— Kalakaua Boathouse —
way cool exhibits —
history of tattoos,
history of surfing —
full humpback
whale skeleton —
Aloha Tower — by
harbor — slooooow
elevator, great view

My fingers were starting to hurt. I was near the end of my second thirty-six-exposure roll of film.

I took a writing break as we walked along the row of shops that line the waterfront.

That was gorgeous. I clicked away.

We detoured up Merchant Street, passing some old-fashioned buildings that seemed out of place. We ended up in Chinatown for lunch, where I had something called Szechuan chicken.

It was great, even though I didn't recognize everything on my plate. "What's this?" I asked, popping a little, shiny, vegetable-ish thing into my mouth.

"Jessi, that's a dried hot pepper!" Claudia cried out. "Don't even think of — "

Gulp.

Take this warning from me. Never swallow a dried hot pepper. You will be taking your life in your hands. I cannot tell you how awful it felt. I thought my throat would explode. I drank about a gallon of ice water. I reserved one line in Mal's book for the unique experience:

Yeeeeeoouch!

Claudia was so cruel. She grabbed my camera and took a photo of me guzzling water. I'm sure steam was puffing out of my ears.

I did not feel much better until our group headed back to the waterfront arcade. There we ate mango ice cream in an outdoor cafe near the Aloha Tower.

Well, we didn't all eat mango ice cream.

Claudia is now eating a banana split with four different flavors of ice cream, butterscotch and hot fudge sauces, whipped cream, chopped pineapples, and crushed macadamia nuts.

Rong! Its only three difrent flavers of ice creme. They cheated me.

Of course, I snapped before-and-after shots of Claudia and the Disappearing Dessert.

Afterward, Mrs. Hall took us to an outdoor hula festival. I scampered around the area, finding dramatic angles for photos.

As we walked back to the hotel, Mary Anne spun around. "I feel sooooo relaxed!"

Everyone around her agreed.

Except me. I was exhausted.

Oh, well. I'd done my job. At least Mallory would know how our vacation really felt. I could always ask her.

CHAPTER 5

Mallory
☺

Tuesday

It feels funny writing in the BSC notebook when most of the club is so far away. But you know me. Dedicated and loyal.

Besides, Kristy would kill me if I didn't.

Anyway, Farm Camp has been a lot of work, but it's so much fun. Karen's friend Tia is visiting from Nebraska, and she's joined the camp. Now all the kids are busy preparing for the county fair on Friday.

As for baby-sitting, well, Kristy and I are running the show. Even though a lot of clients are on vacation, we're working hard. Kristy makes me wear the new BSC T-shirt to every job. I don't mind that, though.

Every once in awhile, I have to admit, I wish I were far, far away. Like maybe in Hawaii.

For example, today . . .

"*SHE'S NOT! SHE'S NOT! SHE'S NOT! SHE'S NOT!*" Jenny Prezzioso was lying on the kitchen floor, stamping her feet and shrieking.

Mrs. Prezzioso was standing at the table, looking at her.

I knew what the next step would be. Mrs. P. would pick Jenny up, give her a big kiss, and take some ice cream out of the freezer. Or take candy out of the cupboard. Or promise to buy Jenny a new doll, or a video, or whatever other thing she wanted at that moment.

Jenny, as you can guess, is spoiled. She has more possessions than any other four-year-old child I know. Personally, I think Toys "R" Us should install a tunnel directly to Jenny's house. That way the Prezziosos wouldn't have to spend money on gas.

"*SHE'S NOT! SHE'S NOT! SHE'S NOT! SHE'S NOT!*"

In case you were wondering, the "SHE" Jenny was yelling about was me. The "NOT" was as in "NOT GOING TO BABY-SIT."

What did she have against me? I had no idea. We'd always gotten along well before. But with Jenny, you never know.

Anyway, I was wrong about Mrs. P. She didn't do any of the things I expected her to do.

"Mallory," she said softly. "Please come into the living room with me."

I followed her away from Tropical Storm Jenny. We huddled together in a quiet corner.

"My husband and I have been involved in a parenting group," she said in a low voice. "We've learned so much from the professionals and other parents. You see, we've been giving Jenny too much power. . . ."

(I did not say, "I could have told you that." I held myself back.)

"So we've started setting limits," Mrs. P. went on. "As you can tell, Jenny is in rebellion. She's been throwing tantrums like this all week. We've discovered that the best thing to do is ignore her. Compassionately, though. We say, 'Jenny, when you're finished, you may come and tell us,' and then we walk away. She fusses and fumes for a few minutes, then stops. She works it out all by herself. I'd like you to follow this method, okay, Mallory?"

I nodded politely, but inside I was dancing with joy. Jenny needed discipline like this. "Sure."

Jenny's protest was already quieting down.

Mrs. P. smiled. "Don't take it personally — what she was saying. She still likes you, Mal. Anyway, Andrea's sleeping. Jenny just had a big lunch, so she can have a snack around three o'clock, but no sweets."

"Okay," I said, taking mental notes.

" 'Bye. Good luck."

Mrs. P. went into the kitchen and said goodbye to Jenny. Then she swept out the front door.

When I entered the kitchen, Jenny was sitting on a kitchen chair, doodling on a notepad with crayons. "Hi, Jenny!" I said.

"It's *Jennifer*, that's my name," she replied.

"Oh! Sorry. What're you doing?"

"Making a beautiful picture. But it's not for you."

"Eeeeeeeee!" Andrea's voice wafted into the room.

I scooted into the nursery. Andrea was squirming in her bassinet, waking up.

"Hello there!" I said. "Do you need a little diaper change?"

"She can't answer you," Jenny yelled from the kitchen. "She's a baby!"

"Thank you," I called out.

I changed Andrea's diaper and brought her into the kitchen. Unlike her sister, Andrea was in a great mood. She burbled and chattered in baby syllables.

"She's saying she wants to drink her bottle," Jenny reported. "She already had yucky baby food for lunch."

I set Andrea in a high chair and quickly prepared her bottle.

"I want ice cream," Jenny announced.

"Maybe after dinner tonight," I replied. "Your mom said — "

"NO! I WANT ICE CREAM NOOOOWWW!"

"Jenny — I mean, Jennifer — "

She fell to the floor again. *"I HATE YOU, YOU STUPID! YOU GIVE ANDREA WHAT-EVER SHE WANTS! I HATE YOU! I HATE YOU! I HATE YOU!"*

"WAAAAAAHHH!" Andrea shrieked.

I ran to Andrea and picked her up. The bottle seemed to quiet her down, but Jenny was a lost cause. She was wailing away.

I gritted my teeth and remembered Mrs. P.'s advice.

"Jennifer," I shouted, "I'm going outside with your sister now! When you're finished, you can join us if you want!"

"IIII HAAAATE YOUUUUUU!"

I went into the backyard and sat in a lounge chair under a big tree. Calmly I fed Andrea.

Inside, Jenny carried on even more loudly. Much more loudly. I half expected the neighbors to dial 911.

Mad as I was, I had a strong urge to go back inside and comfort her. Sure, she was being obnoxious, but she also seemed to be so unhappy.

Well, no police arrived. And Jenny's screaming soon turned into whimpers, then stopped.

A few minutes later she bounced outside with her art project. "Look what I made!"

She held out a sheet of white paper with circles and squiggles in many different colors.

"Wow," I said. "That's beautiful."

"It's for you. It's a garden with big flowers and a huge gigantic bear eating them."

"Ohhhhh, I see."

"Can we go to the park and play in the sprinkler?"

"Sure," I replied.

"Yeeeaaaaa!"

Andrea was just about finished with her bottle. I sat with her a little longer, then brought her inside. Quickly I helped Jenny pick out a bathing suit, then darted to the kitchen to pack some provisions in the diaper bag — apple–cinnamon mini rice cakes, a box of crackers, a full bottle.

I was back outside, fastening Andrea in her stroller and tying a bonnet on her head, when

Jenny emerged. She was wearing a tiara and cape, and she held a magic wand in her right hand. "I'm going to make the park into an enchanted world of deep discounts!"

"Uh, excuse me?"

"That means toys and games," Jenny explained. "I saw it on TV. This fairy goes into an empty room and waves her wand and makes toys appear. At the lowest possible price."

"Oh, right," I said.

We shoved off in the direction of the park.

The day had really heated up. I was sweating by the time we arrived. The sprinkler was going full force, and kids were crowded underneath. (Boy, was I tempted to join them.)

As Jenny scampered into the spray, tiara and all, I wheeled Andrea to a shady bench. I sat near a woman who was reading a paperback novel.

I played with Andrea for awhile, keeping an eye on Jenny. An ice cream truck pulled up to a nearby corner and played a tinkly, music-box-type tune. I stood Andrea on my lap and made her dance to the beat. She thought that was hilarious.

"Mallory, come here!" Jenny shouted.

She was playing in the sandbox now. Her wet body was coated with sand. I picked up Andrea and walked over to Jenny.

"I want a Fudgsicle!" she demanded.

"Well, I have apple–cinnamon mini rice cakes," I said.

"Yuck! I hate those! Those are poison! Buy me a Fudgsicle. I'll wash my hands."

"Jennifer, your mom told me you weren't to have any sweets — "

"I DON'T WANT SWEETS! I WANT ICE CREAM!"

I had a few dollars in my pocket. Enough for an ice cream for both of us. But I held firm.

"Sorry, Jennifer."

"YOU'RE NOT MY MOMMY! MOMMY WOULD LET ME! YOU'RE STUPID AND I HATE YOU!" Jenny picked up a fistful of sand. Before she could throw it, I turned my back. Sand rained around me, but none of it landed on Andrea.

I was furious. I marched back to the bench and sat down.

Jenny stood up and began kicking sand all over the place. (Fortunately, no kids were near her.) She threw her magic wand across the playground. Her features scrunched up. She burst into tears.

Tinkle-de-tinkle-de-tinkle-de-tinkle went the bells of the ice cream truck.

I wanted to throw a rock at it.

"AAAAAAAAAAAAAAAAGGHHHHHH!" A shriek ripped out of Jenny's mouth. She threw

herself onto the sand, kicking her feet and flailing her arms.

A mom passed by, holding a toddler. She cast a startled look toward Jenny, then saw me and walked on. Another mom gave me a tiny smile. I didn't know if she was being sympathetic or polite or just glad her kids weren't such monsters.

The woman beside me set down her book and stared at Jenny. I felt mortified. I imagined the whole park was staring at us. Plus the ice-cream man. Plus the people who lived across the street.

But I was not going to let that bother me. Jenny was in no danger. She was putting no other kids in danger. I was determined to leave her there. She had to learn.

"She seems to be in great pain," said the woman with the book.

I turned toward her. She was looking at me very sternly.

"Well, I know," I replied. "But her mom said — "

"I'm sure her mom doesn't mean for her child to be neglected, dear."

Neglected? How could she say that? What did she know about dealing with spoiled brats?

"Thanks," I said politely.

I did not budge an inch. I continued playing with Andrea.

"YOOUUU'RE STUUUUPIIIID!" Jenny shrieked.

The woman slapped her book shut and stood up. Shaking her head and muttering to herself, she began to walk away.

I tried not to look at her, but I couldn't help it. She had stopped, and she was glaring at me.

Well, not at me, exactly.

She was reading the print on my shirt. The Baby-sitters Club's name and number.

CHAPTER 6

Claudia

Wendsday

Today I went with a bunch of kids on a side trip to the Perl City area. We went to a musiam and saw a movie. It was fasin fastonot intresting. I reccomend it. Hope your having fun at Farm Camp, Mallery!

U_{gh.}

That came out sounding so dull.

But I couldn't help it. I was still kind of in shock. I didn't dare write about how I was really feeling.

The day started out fine. It was clear and gorgeous (again). We all woke up early (again) and had a fantastic, delicious breakfast in the hotel (again).

Well, most of it was fantastic and delicious.

I would not, however, touch the Samoan Baked Breadfruit with *Pe'e Pe'e.*

"Claudia, it's wonderful," Dawn insisted as we passed down the line.

"Are you crazy?" I said. "It sounds disgusting! The breadfruit's bad enough. How do you know what's in it?"

Dawn laughed. "The word has apostrophes! It's pronounced *peh-eh peh-eh.* It's made with coconut cream."

"How can you be sure?"

I didn't listen to Dawn's answer. It's a free country, and I stuck with the simpler stuff.

After breakfast, we split into groups again. As usual, most kids wanted to go to the beach. I was leaning in that direction, too. But Ms. Bernhardt, my social studies teacher, offered to take a group to Pearl City to visit Pearl Harbor.

I signed up right away.

Once, when I was a little girl, I was on vacation with my family when an awful man started arguing with my dad. I don't recall what they were fighting about, but I do remember the man saying something like, "You got us at Pearl Harbor. What more do you want?"

And I'll never forget my dad's reaction. His face went cold. He turned and walked away without saying another word, signaling for us to follow.

I realized that the man had said something bigoted to Dad, but I couldn't figure out what.

I asked Janine soon afterward, and she told me.

You see, many years ago, Japanese warplanes sneak-attacked the U.S. naval base at Pearl Harbor. They destroyed huge ships and killed thousands of sailors. That was what finally drove the United States to enter World War Two. After the attack, anti-Japanese prejudice was tremendous in the U.S. Thousands of innocent Japanese-American citizens were sent away to isolated, prison-like places called internment camps, for no other reason than their ethnicity. (I read about all this in a book called *A Fence Away from Freedom* by Ellen Levine, which has interviews with people who were sent to the camps as kids.)

It was hard to imagine something as awful as the bombing in a place like Hawaii. I was curious to see Pearl Harbor firsthand.

We took the public bus. I sat with Mary Anne, who was the only other BSC member to sign up (four boys did, too).

When we arrived, Ms. Bernhardt led us through an entrance gate, where the guard gave her a number.

"Listen up," Ms. Bernhardt announced. "We are going to see the remains of the battleship *USS Arizona*, but we have to take a shuttle boat to reach it. We're in the next group, so let's hit the museum in the meantime."

I didn't see any bomb craters. I saw plenty of sailors walking around. Everything looked in good shape. I was glad Pearl Harbor had recovered.

In the museum we saw exhibits about the Japanese-American soldiers who had fought for the U.S. in World War Two. That was cool.

Then our number was called, and we were ushered into a movie theater. "I didn't know we were going to see a movie," Mary Anne whispered.

"Did you spot a popcorn stand?" I asked.

"No."

We both giggled as the lights went down. I did not giggle after that. I couldn't. The

movie was sickening. Someone had actually filmed the destruction of Pearl Harbor. You could hear the bombers buzzing overhead and see the ships exploding into bits, sending huge chunks of metal into the air.

Over two thousand American servicemen died in the attack. Six battleships were sunk in the harbor. Three hundred warplanes were destroyed.

By Japan.

Hearing about it had been bad enough. Seeing it made me sick to my stomach.

My parents hadn't been born then. But my grandparents were living in Japan. I remember my grandmother telling me that everyone in Japan used to revere the emperor. But the emperor had ordered the attack. So did that mean my grandparents were in favor of it? How had they reacted to the news? With happiness? Triumph?

The thought was horrifying. *My* grandmother? Sweet, kind Mimi?

Why? Why did the emperor do it? The film didn't really explain.

When the lights went up, I was shaking.

As we walked out, a guide led us toward the shuttle boat. We piled aboard, with a few dozen other tourists.

Floating in the bay in front of us was a huge, rectangular concrete building that sagged in the middle. It looked like a bar of cream cheese that someone had tried to squash.

It did not, however, look like the remains of a ship.

Then, as we drew closer, I could see twisted, rusty black pieces of metal jutting out of the water.

"That's what is left of the *Arizona*," Ms. Bernhardt said. "One of the strongest ships ever built."

"Cool," said Pete Black, who was in our group.

I didn't think it was cool at all. I thought of all the sailors who had been inside, not knowing what was in store for them, hearing a strange buzzing noise that grew louder and louder . . .

Cool? Horrible was more like it. Outrageous. Unthinkable.

Our boat docked alongside the memorial, and we stepped aboard. Our guide was an elderly man named Mr. Blanchard, who was wearing a U.S. Navy hat. He led us through the museum inside, which contained a small chapel. On the wall of the chapel was a marble tablet carved with the names of the servicemen who died on that long-ago day in Pearl Harbor.

Mr. Blanchard paused by a big window.

Outside it, a piece of the *Arizona* stuck up from the water like a burned, bony hand.

"I am a Pearl Harbor survivor," Mr. Blanchard announced. "I was stationed here in nineteen forty-one when the attack occurred."

Our entire group, SMS kids and tourists, fell silent. Mr. Blanchard looked out the window and said softly, "I was one of the lucky ones. It was a Sunday, and I was on leave. But I lost some of my best buddies right here. The *Arizona*, as you can see, is still underneath us. And so are they."

My heart did a flip-flop.

Oh my lord. Underneath us? The idea was so morbid I started feeling dizzy. How did Mr. Blanchard ever get over the horror? And what about the sailors' families?

The poor guys never had a chance. They were ambushed.

And everyone in that group knew who'd done the ambushing.

I stared straight ahead. I knew I wasn't the only Asian there that day. But were any of the others Japanese-American? Would people know that I was? Or would they take me for Hawaiian, or Korean, or Chinese?

Mimi once told me about a friend of hers, a little girl who'd immigrated to America around the same time she did. The girl wanted so badly to look like a Caucasian, she walked around everywhere with her eyes wide open, thinking she'd fool people.

Janine and I used to roll on the floor with laughter whenever we heard that story. Our parents raised us to be proud of our heritage. And I always have been.

Until that day.

I could not stop thinking of that little girl. For the first time in my life, I wished I had blond hair and round blue eyes. I felt the eyes of the people in our group burning into the back of my head.

"Claudia?" Mary Anne asked. "Are you okay?"

For a moment — just a moment — I thought I'd tell Mary Anne what I was thinking. But I couldn't. This was something I had to keep inside me.

"Fine!" I replied. "Just a little . . . seasick, that's all."

As we walked on, following Mr. Blanchard and Ms. Bernhardt, I thought of Hiroshima and Nagasaki. About the atomic bombs that flattened those entire cities. The bombs were dropped by the U.S. That was much worse than this.

But thinking about that didn't make me feel better at all. In fact, it made me feel worse.

The whole war, when you thought about it, was a terrible, bloody mess. It should never have been started in the first place.

I could not wait to get far, far away from Pearl Harbor.

CHAPTER 7

Abby

Wednesday

Two days in Waikiki. Sunning on the beach. Swimming. Browsing in local shops.

What a life. I could stay here forever.

Maybe I will. After I become a big Hollywood star, of course. Then I'll have my own *private jet, with enough seats for everyone in the BSC. Note to Kristy: I know what you're thinking. But don't worry, I will arrange for mobile phones in case we fly on a Monday, Wednesday, or Friday at 5:30...*

"Have you seen a record store?" Stacey asked.

I riffled through my Hawaiian phrase book. "*Ewa*."

"Ay vah?" Stacey asked.

"*Ewa*. That means 'away from Diamond Head.' That's how you give directions here. *Ewa* and *Diamond Head*."

Diamond Head, by the way, is an extinct volcano. It's just past Waikiki.

Which is where Stacey and I were on Wednesday morning (Waikiki, not the volcano), along with Mrs. Gonzalez and eight other SMS kids.

75

Abby

Yes, Waikiki has a beach, and no, we were not on it. Did you think this trip was pure laziness and fun? Guess again. We were examining the local customs and native habitats.

Well, sort of. We were shopping on Waikiki's main drag, Kalakaua Avenue.

To tell you the truth, just about all of Waikiki is a shopping district. Except for the beach.

The beach is another story. I'd spent part of Tuesday there, so I knew it well.

Look to your right and you see sand, sand, sand. In front of you are hundreds of swimmers, surfers, and windsurfers. Diamond Head is to your left, like a distant crouching monster.

Behind you are the high-rise hotels (speaking of monsters). They're like a bunch of ugly giant androids, elbowing each other for the best view of the ocean.

Or I should say, best view of the *moana*, in the Hawaiian tongue.

"Abby, will you take your head out of that book?" Stacey said. "We don't have — "

"Also, you don't say north or south," I told her. "You say *mauka* when you mean toward the mountains, and *makai* when you mean toward the ocean."

"Abby*yyy* — "

" 'Pidgin English is another dialect spoken by the locals,' " I read. " 'It has a rich vocabulary all its own.' "

"I'm leaving," Stacey said.

I closed the book. "Sorry. Shall we look at some hideous Hawaiian shirts?"

Stacey gave me stinkeye (loosely translated: a Look, in pidgin English). She did not seem terribly interested in the goods at the Hula Souvenir Shoppe. Mrs. Gonzalez had allowed us half an hour to browse on our own before we met up again, and I think Stacey had grander things in mind.

Stacey was WOR (WithOut Robert) this morning, because he hates shopping. So I think she felt pressure to do a whole week's worth right then.

As for me? Well, I have to confess a deep, dark secret. I loooove tacky, touristy shops. I don't know why. My mom calls me a tsotchke maven (loosely translated from the Yiddish: someone who loves weird and cheap trinkets).

Before Stacey could say a word, I picked up a small, windup hula dancer. I turned its key, and it started singing "Aloha 'Oe."

"I absolutely have to buy this!" I exclaimed.

Stacey was history. Off on a quest for Ralph Lauren.

I ended up with a tin pineapple pencil sharpener, a glow-in-the-dark Waikiki plastic tumbler, and a poster of a grumpy-looking bulldog that said I'D RATHER BE WIND-SURFING.

Abby

Afterward our group headed east — er, *Diamond Head* — toward peaceful Kapiolani Park. There we heard a guy playing a guitar, which makes funny, swooping sounds (if you've ever heard "Aloha 'Oe," you know what I mean). Next stop was the Waikiki Aquarium, where we saw coral that looked like tentacled extraterrestrial beasts. (Did you know that coral is a living thing? I didn't.) I also enjoyed watching these cute Hawaiian monk seals, until a guard told us they were on the brink of extinction. (I'm glad Dawn wasn't there. She'd have organized a protest on the spot.)

The moment we left the building, Stacey cried out, "Tanning time!"

"You've all had enough of this strenuous trip?" Mrs. Gonzalez asked.

"Yeeaaahh!"

It was unanimous. We marched *makai*. Mrs. Gonzalez rented an umbrella and we hit the beach.

Well, "hit" isn't exactly the right word. "Stepped gingerly between towels" was more like it. Finding a spot for ten kids and a grown-up on Waikiki Beach is a little like finding a seat on the New York City subway at rush hour.

"Follow me." I led everybody toward the edge of the beach, farthest from the hotels. It was definitely a better choice: more room, less noise, and lots of hunky surfers running around.

I spread out my towel *surfer* (in the direction of the surfers). Stacey put hers to my right.

I slathered myself with the highest-possible-power sunscreen. I breathed in the warm, salty air and smiled.

"No allergies?" Stacey asked.

"Nope," I replied as I lay down.

I was in total heaven.

I must have dozed off, because when I opened my eyes, Stacey was gone.

I stood up. Mrs. Gonzalez was under the umbrella with her nose in a magazine. Some of the other kids were throwing a Frisbee around. I spotted Stacey in the water.

I was about to join her when a volleyball landed at my feet.

"Sorry!" a voice called out.

I picked up the ball, threw it upward, and punched it. It sailed into the arms of a blond, dimply guy with muscular pecs. "Good shot," he said.

"Thanks," I replied.

But I was looking over his shoulder. At a TV camera crew, setting up by a volleyball net.

A dark-haired woman wearing a backward-turned baseball cap was pacing around, shouting into a mobile phone. Two volleyball teams faced off across the net. When Mr.

Dimples returned, they started playing.

I don't know about you, but I absolutely adore volleyball.

I especially adore it when TV cameras are nearby.

Did I ever tell you I was on TV once? Yup. I was in fifth grade, and a local news team came to cover a hurricane that blew a tree into our school. I was the girl crossing her eyes behind the newscaster, just to the left. (I saved the tape. I play it, oh, twice a month. I think it shows real talent.)

Anyway, as I moseyed over to the volleyball net, I could hear what the woman was saying into the phone: "She should have told us she was union. What am I going to do now?"

I watched the teams volley for awhile. When the ball bounced into the sidelines, I bumped it back in.

The woman closed the phone and stormed over to the court area. "Guys," she said, "we have a delay. One of the actors can't do the job. Another one has an audition and can't make it until tomorrow. The commercial won't look right without full teams. I'm going to have to call the client and ask . . ."

I was beginning to see stars.

I was just as good a player as any of the actors. Okay, not as old or as tall, but who says volleyball team members have to look alike?

I slipped closer to the net. I turned slightly to my right (that's my good side). I did not want to be obnoxious. Just subtle. Let them discover me.

"So we'll wrap it until tomorrow morning," the woman said.

"I can play!" I blurted out.

Ugh. Subtle as a steamroller.

The woman hardly looked at me. "Uh-huh — "

"Seriously," I said. "I'm on my school team. I've also been on TV."

(All right, SMS doesn't have a volleyball team — but the last part was true, sort of.)

Now everyone was paying attention. "How old are you?" the woman asked.

"Eighteen," I lied.

"Are you union?"

Huh?

"Uh — well — no, not yet, but — " I spluttered.

"Good. This is a nonunion commercial, for Day-Nite suntan lotion — "

"My favorite!" I exclaimed. (I had never heard of it.)

"Let's see you play a little."

I lined up with my fellow actors. Mr. Dimples tossed me the ball and I served.

We volleyed. I bumped. I set. I positioned myself wisely. I even spiked one.

"Okay, fine," the woman said. "You're perfect. Can you make it tomorrow morning at seven-thirty?"

"Oh, yeah, to me it's, like, something like, I don't know, twelve-thirty or so? So yeah, I'll be wide awake," I blathered.

"Okay, come over here and let me take down your name and phone number."

"Hey, congrats!" Mr. Dimples called out.

"Thanks!" I shouted.

Perfect. She'd said I was perfect!

I was floating. I could not feel my feet touch the ground. I, Abby Stevenson, was going to be in a major TV commercial.

I figured Mr. Kingbridge would need to okay this. But I wasn't worried a bit. He'd understand. He's human.

Besides, I could always sneak away.

This was a big break. Winona Ryder started in commercials. Meryl Streep. Katharine Hepburn. (Actually, I'm just guessing about them, but I know lots of actors did.)

Okay, maybe it wasn't a big break. But it was a first step. And you have to take a step before you run up the mountaintop.

I could already picture my name inside a star on Hollywood Boulevard.

CHAPTER 8

Dawn

Wednesday

Whew. I finally got this book from Jessi. I thought she'd never let go.

~~Very funny~~.

Just kidding. Anyway, Mal, I figured you'd want to hear about the unspoiled Hawaii. The natural part, far away from the hustle and bustle of the city.

Today Jessi and I almost went to the beach. But we changed our minds when Mr. Wong agreed to take a group on a side tour into the heart of wild, volcanic Oahu...

"**O**hhhhh, this is beautiful," Jessi said.

Jessi raised her camera to the open window. Our van's engine groaned as we swerved up a mountain road. Outside, the city of Honolulu was swinging into view in the distance.

Inside, my stomach was threatening to hurl my breakfast into the woods.

Jessi, Logan, and I had joined a group called "Off the Beaten Track," led by Mr. Wong, an SMS art teacher. Altogether, ten of us were heading to the top of Mount Tantalus, Honolulu's highest point.

Click! Jessi photographed the city in the distance.

Click! Jessi photographed the beautiful homes along the road.

Click! Jessi photographed me, looking like the ghost of the Hawaiian Barf Beast.

"Jessi, have a heart," I pleaded.

"Sorry," Jessi said.

"Are you all right?" Mr. Wong asked. "Would you like me to tell the van driver to stop?"

"I — I think so," I murmured.

"Uh-oh, grab the bucket," remarked Austin Bentley, an eighth-grade boy I had never hated until that moment.

I felt so embarrassed. I used to have car-sickness as a little girl. I thought I'd recovered for life. Boy, was I wrong.

I felt the van slowing down. Mr. Wong was leaning toward me with a warm, sympathetic smile. "We're almost there," he said. "We'll pull into the parking lot in a minute. Dawn, you can get out first."

As the van came to a stop, I wobbled toward the front on shaky legs. Mr. Wong helped me step down to the parking lot.

I was hit by a blast of cold air (well, cold for Hawaii). Fortunately, we'd been warned to wear our windbreakers. I zipped mine up tight.

Overhead, palm trees bent in the wind. Tourists in T-shirts and shorts shivered as they walked past us toward a lookout point.

I leaned against a tree.

"Take a picture, take a picture!" Austin called out.

"Knock it off, Austin," Jessi said.

You know what? The air of Mount Tantalus was curing me. Totally. I felt so good, I clutched my stomach in pretend pain, blew my cheeks out, and ran after Austin.

I have never seen a boy look so scared or run so fast.

The view from the lookout point? Stunning.

In L.A., I sometimes ride with my dad up to the Santa Monica Mountains. We always stop at the top and look out over Los Angeles — or what we can see of it. Usually it's covered in a thick, greenish-brown haze of smog.

Here in Hawaii, though, the air was so fresh and cool, it was like drinking water from a stream. Below us, Honolulu and Diamond Head were crystal clear. If I looked hard enough, I was sure I could see Claudia and Mary Anne in Pearl Harbor, Abby and Stacey in Waikiki.

Jessi, of course, was snapping away.

"How many rolls of film have you taken?" asked Logan.

"Nine," Jessi replied.

Next she took a small cassette recorder out of her pocket and held it up to her mouth. "Hi, Mal. Hear the wind? We're on top of Mount Tantalus, which is about two thousand feet above sea level . . ."

Jessi was just finishing up her monologue when Mr. Wong called us back to the van.

I dreaded going inside again. (Austin didn't sit anywhere near me.) But as we wound our way down the other side of the mountain, I didn't feel a twinge of sickness.

For one thing, the road down was a little smoother. For another, the countryside was taking my breath away. Especially when we drove through the gates of a place called Paradise Park. It was as if the ground had exploded with trees and fiery, vibrant flowers. A light rain was falling, which seemed to make it all sparkle.

"This is Manoa Valley," Mr. Wong told us. "It's called the last urban rain forest."

"How do you spell Manoa?" Jessi asked, scribbling away in her notebook.

"Jessi, just *look*!" I finally said.

As the van pulled to another stop, Logan held up a guidebook and called out excitedly, "This place was founded by a guy named James Wong!"

Mr. Wong beamed. "Well, um, I try to keep this a secret, you see, modest fellow that I am . . ."

We gave Mr. Wong grief about his "private garden" all day.

For lunch we ate in the Treetop Restaurant, which is actually built in . . . a treetop! (Jessi, of course, took pictures from below and above.)

"So," Jessi said as she sat down at the table again, "are you glad you came on the trip?"

I smiled. I hadn't planned on this trip to Hawaii. In June I'd traveled from my home in California to spend the summer in Stoneybrook. When the idea for the Hawaii trip came up, I thought, no way. Pay for another fare, fly back across the country, turn around and go back to Connecticut, and then to California again, in one summer? It seemed ridiculous. All along I'd felt a little guilty about saying yes.

Now, looking over the rain forest, sipping tea and eating sandwiches, my doubts had flown away.

"Yeah," I said. "I can't imagine being anywhere else."

In that pleasant atmosphere, Austin Bentley almost choked on a baconburger. (Serves him right, the carnivore.) He coughed a few times, then pointed to a spot behind me.

I turned around. The sun was peeking through the branches of the palms. Birds dived and floated, their red, blue, and orange plumage flashing in the light.

And through it all was a long, arching rainbow.

"Wow . . ." Jessi murmured.

I will never forget that sight. I felt as if we had been transported to the beginning of time.

Well, except for the *click-click-click*ing of a camera in the seat beside me.

CHAPTER 9

Kristy

Wednesday

What a day. I don't know how you guys are doing over in Hawaii, but here at Farm Camp, life is tough.

Karen's friend Lia is sweet, but she's become totally New Yorkified. When I told her about you, Stacey, she begged me to ask you to come home.

I told her I would. She made me write you a postcard in front of her. If you got it, Stace, I hope you ignored it. Otherwise, I guess I may see you at the county fair next Friday. . . .

"I'm going to waaake up in the city that never sweeeeeps . . ." sang Tia Farrell.

"I think that's *'sleeps,'* " I said. "The city that never *sleeps*."

Tia laughed. "No, silly! Everyone knows a city can't sleep. It's *sweeps*, because of all the garbage on the streets."

"Beeeeeeah!" bleated Oliver Twist.

"Ti*aaaa*," Karen called out. "Pay attention."

Oliver Twist, by the way, is a lamb. Tia is a girl. A girl who was raised on a big farm in Nebraska and is supposed to know how to bottle-feed a lamb.

What was she doing instead? Putting a styrofoam Statue of Liberty hat on Ollie's head and serenading him with "New York, New York."

Why was she doing this? Well, think about it. If you lived in a big city, where would you want to go for the summer? The country, right? Well, I guess it's the other way around for a farm girl.

Tia was not too interested in being at Farm Camp during her vacation from the farm. She wanted bright lights and action. So, over the weekend, Watson had taken her and Karen to New York City.

And Tia still hadn't recovered.

The problem was, Farm Camp was a lot of

work. The Stones' farm is not exactly a huge ponderosa, but it has a couple of horses and cows, some pigs and chickens, two geese, a goat named Elvira, and Oliver Twist.

As you can imagine, caring for those animals takes a lot of time and effort. And that was the point of Farm Camp. Help Mrs. Stone, learn about the farm, and have fun. Plus the county fair was approaching, and we were preparing a few projects for it — a piece of needlework, some homegrown vegetables for the produce contest, a recipe for a bake-off.

And Oliver Twist.

He was going to be Karen's entry in the livestock contest. So feeding and pampering him was extremely important.

"This bag upon shoes . . ." Tia sang, finally inserting the bottle into Ollie's mouth, "are longing to stay . . ."

It's *vagabond shoes*. And longing to *stray*. But I didn't say anything. Out of the corner of my eye, I spotted a group of kids trashing the vegetable garden.

"Linny, stop!" Mallory was shouting. "What are you doing?"

Linny Papadakis stalked away, smashing a few fallen tomatoes beneath his feet. "She's being a baby!" he shouted.

Linny's little sister, Hannie, was crying.

"My yellow squash is bigger than his," she said.

"Is not!" Linny retorted.

"He tried to pick it, so his would grow bigger!" Hannie protested.

"Hannie's is bigger, Hannie's is bigger," Patsy Kuhn taunted.

"Look, *beans*!" Laurel Kuhn squealed, cutting across the eggplant patch.

I ran toward the garden, shouting, "Guys, be careful!"

"We are all growing these together," Mallory patiently explained to Linny.

"But I *called* the yellow squash plants first," Linny insisted.

"Beeeeeah!" said Ollie.

I turned around, and Tia and Karen were nowhere to be seen. Poor Ollie was wandering around in his pen, looking thirsty and abandoned.

"Karen! Tia!" I called out.

No answer.

I picked up Ollie's bottle and fed him some more, while Mallory calmed the garden wars. It was a hot day, and Ollie sucked down the rest of the bottle in no time.

"Still thirsty, huh?" I asked.

"Beeeah," Ollie replied.

"Okay, stay right there." I ran inside to the kitchen.

As I filled the bottle with milk, I could hear "Jingle Bells" coming from the living room.

I took a detour in that direction. Karen and Tia were in front of the TV, watching intently.

"What are you guys doing?" I asked.

"There's Macy's!" Tia blurted out. "I was there!"

It took me a minute to realize what they were watching. *"Miracle on Thirty-Fourth Street?"* I asked. "In July?"

"It's a New York movie," Karen informed me. "Tia wants to see all the New York movies ever made. We already saw *Home Alone 2* at our house."

I picked up the remote and flicked the set off. "Sorry, camp's not — "

"Oh, boo!" Karen said. "That's not fair."

"Kristy? Can you help me out here?" Mallory's voice called from outside.

"We'll ask Mrs. Stone if we can borrow the tape," I said. "Now out out *out!*"

Well, needless to say, Mal and I were not exactly full of energy at our BSC meeting that night.

BSD meeting would have been more like it. Baby-sitters Duo.

"Uh, I call this meeting to order," I said at five-thirty.

Mallory was lying face-up on Claudia's bed. "It already is, isn't it?"

"Well, I guess, but I have to say it."

"Kristy, this feels so weird."

"I know."

We both giggled. And then we both fell silent. You know what I wanted more than anything else? I wanted Claudia to be there, so she could burrow somewhere and pull out some junk food. With her gone, Mal and I just couldn't bring ourselves to do it. It didn't seem right.

"Kristy," Mallory finally said, sitting up. "Do you think it's wrong to ignore a kid's tantrum?"

"Claire's going through a phase, huh?"

"Not Claire. Just answer me. Your honest opinion."

"Well, it depends on the age of the kid, whether she's in danger, what the parents say — "

"But what about in a public place, like a playground?" Mal continued. "Is it bad to let the kid scream and yell?"

"You know kids. They do that in public places because they *know* they'll get attention. It embarrasses parents. Which is kind of dumb. I mean, why be embarrassed? All the other parents have seen tantrums before.

They won't be scandalized by a kid being ignored."

"I'm not so sure about that."

"Mallory, who are we talking about?"

"Jenny Prezzioso. Yesterday her mom told me to ignore her tantrums and let them boil over."

"Really? It's about time."

"So when I took the kids to the park and Jenny threw a fit in the sandbox, I did just that," Mal said. "But some woman started yelling at me."

"Who?"

Mallory shrugged. "I'd never seen her before in my life."

"She had no right telling you what to do!"

"I was so ashamed, Kristy. She told me I was neglecting Jenny."

"Mallory, you were being a good sitter," I insisted. "First of all, you were just doing what you were told. Second of all, you knew it was the right thing to do. That old busybody should have minded her own business."

"I wish you'd been there. You should have seen the look she gave me — "

Rrrrring!

I picked up the receiver. "Hello, Baby-sitters Club."

"Yes, hello, my name is Margaret Wellfleet. I called yesterday and the answering machine directed me to call today between five-thirty and six. I'd like to speak to the person in charge of your organization."

"That's me," I said.

"Your name?"

Uh-oh. I did not like the sound of this voice. "Kristin Thomas," I replied.

"Well, Miss Thomas, I suggest that if you intend to advertise your organization on shirts, you be sure that those shirts are worn by competent child care personnel."

I gave Mallory a Look. Silently I mouthed, *It's her*!

Mallory swallowed hard. The color drained from her face.

"Well, thank you," I said politely into the phone, "but all of our sitters are trained and experienced — "

"Then perhaps you ought to reexamine your training procedures, because the young woman I saw yesterday had no clue how to care for a young child. She sat on a bench, doing absolutely nothing, while the little girl entrusted to her was screaming and suffering."

"I know exactly who you mean, ma'am," I replied. "She's a good, experienced sitter, and she was only following the instructions of the girl's mother. You see, all children are so different. With some of them, you have to — "

"To what? Ignore them? If the mother had told her to put the child in a cardboard box for three hours, would she have done that, too, Miss Thompson?"

"Thomas. No, of course not, but in this case — "

"Caregivers have minds of their own, too, dear. Children should not be allowed to cry like that. It is humiliating and psychologically harmful. Please don't try to excuse this. This is a case of laziness and neglect. I suggest you remove this young lady from your roster. And if, by some chance, your entire organization believes in this . . . *method*, well, you won't be in business long, I can guarantee that!"

"Okay, Ms. Wellfleet, thank you for calling."

Click.

I stared at the receiver. "She hung up on me."

"Well, you stuck up for me," Mallory said. "Thanks, that was nice."

"I was so polite. I didn't even yell at her. I didn't have a chance to lose my temper and tell her what a nosy creep she was. *She* hung up on *me*."

"What's she going to do, Kristy?" Mallory asked.

"I don't know," I said with a shrug. "Fly away on a broomstick, if we're lucky."

I lowered my face into my hands. This was all we needed. A new enemy in Stoney-brook.

CHAPTER 10

Abby

Thursday

It starts small.
Steven Spielberg
is relaxing in his
penthouse suite at
the Royal Hawaiian
Hotel. He turns on the
TV. He channel-surfs
a bit. All the shows
are boring. He's
ready to turn it off.
But he doesn't.
Suddenly he cannot
take his eyes off

the set. What is it?
A brilliant horror
movie? A moving
new documentary?
    No. A suntan
lotion commercial.
On the surface,
pretty ordinary.
Local teens playing
volleyball. But one
of them is some-
how different. She
seems younger
than the rest. But
she has ... IT. A
certain quality, a
presence, a life
force.
    Hmmm, he thinks.
We haven't yet
found someone to
play the part of the
glamorous thirteen-
year-old asthmatic
in my new movie,
Abigail's Dream. I
wonder who her
agent is ? ...

"Swifty Thomas?" Dawn asked.

"Yes," I replied. "That's who Kristy will be.
Swifty Thomas, hot young agent to the stars.

When Steve calls, I tell him to call the BSC
number between five-thirty and six and ask
for Swifty."

Dawn, Jessi, Mary Anne, and I were eating
our breakfasts. It was seven A.M., a half hour
before I was to report to the beach for the
commercial. I'd been up since five, preparing.
I was full of antihistamines and totally de-
allergized. My hair looked bouncy and clean.
And, to my surprise, not one of my friends
was laughing at my scheme. (I think they were
still half asleep.)

Claudia and Stacey slid in next to us, holding their breakfast trays. "Who's 'Steve'?"
asked Claudia.

"Steven Spielberg," Jessi answered with a
straight face.

Claudia's tray hit the table. "Steven Spielberg is going to call Abby?"

"Well, not yet," Dawn said. "He has to discover her in the TV commercial first."

"Oh." Claudia sank into her seat and began tearing into a ham-and-cheese omelette.
"Don't forget to mention us in your Oscar
speech."

"And give out our number," Jessi added.
"What great publicity."

"Abby won't have to," Dawn remarked.
"Swifty will probably be standing next to her,
holding up a BSC T-shirt."

I lifted my nose in the air. "Scoff if you must. The road to fame and fortune is lined with rubberneckers."

That stopped the conversation flat. "What does *that* mean?" Jessi asked.

"I don't know, I heard it in a movie once." I stood up from the table and put on my backpack, which contained sunscreen and a beach towel.

"Can we come and watch?" Claudia asked.

"You'd better," I replied.

We exchanged good-byes, and I sauntered over to where Ms. Bernhardt was sitting. (I figured, if I was going to be a star, I had to learn to saunter.)

Ms. Bernhardt had agreed to be my escort. She was the only teacher/chaperone who had liked the idea of my doing the commercial. I had brought it up during dinner the night before. Forget about Mr. Kingbridge. He'd started shaking his head even before I'd finished my request.

"This trip is a team effort," he'd said. "We can't have kids running off to do individual things like this."

My angel of fortune, Ms. Bernhardt, had spoken right up. "Oh, Howard, don't be such an old fusspot. How many kids have the chance to do something as exciting as this? I'll be happy to chaperone her. The rest of you can easily handle the groups tomorrow morning."

Old Mr. K. backed right down.

Afterward, when I thanked Ms. Bernhardt, she whispered, "Honey, when I was your age, my daddy wouldn't let me try for a singing career, and I always resented it."

Now, as I approached Ms. Bernhardt, she beamed a big smile. "It's showtime!"

We left the hotel and caught a public bus to Waikiki. At the Diamond Head end of the beach, we got off.

I could spot the camera crew from the road. The workers were fussing with tripods and setting up the volleyball net.

As we walked onto the sand, I felt a little funny. I mean, I'd told them I was eighteen. Why would I need an escort? Were they going to think Ms. Bernhardt was my mom?

It was as if Ms. Bernhardt had read my mind. She whispered, "I brought a beach towel. I'll stay back and hang out on the sand. If anyone suspects anything, I'm your agent. Go ahead. Good luck."

"Thanks," I said.

As I walked to the volleyball net, the angle of the early-morning sun was making me squint. I remembered my sunscreen and took off my backpack to get it.

My hand froze as I pulled it out.

The label said Coppertone. I had told the woman with the phone that Day-Nite was my favorite. What would they do if they saw me using a rival?

I shoved it back in. Hey, it wasn't even seven-thirty. The sun wouldn't really start burning until ten o'clock anyway.

I waved to my fellow actors. "Hi!"

"Hey, it's the new kid on the block!" shouted Mr. Dimples.

The woman who'd been on the phone the day before smiled at me. "Listen, I'm sorry we were so rude yesterday. I'm the director, Kaiulani Flores. Welcome."

One by one, the actors introduced themselves. Mr. Dimples's name was actually Chad. I don't remember all the others, but I do recall a Jim, a Don, a Linda, and a Roxanne.

Poor Roxanne was beet red. She had zinc oxide on her face and wore a T-shirt and long, loose cotton slacks.

I said "Hi" a million times, then stripped down to my bathing suit.

One of the net poles needed to be put up, so I pitched in.

Chad laughed. "What are you doing?"

"Just helping out," I explained.

"You don't do that. That's what the crew is for. You're the talent."

The talent. Yeah, that's what I was. I loved the way that sounded.

When the net was up, we all started playing volleyball. Alongside us, the three camerapeople were still bustling around, running wires, and loading film.

"Listen up, actors," Ms. Flores announced.

We quit playing and gathered near her. I held the ball.

"This shouldn't take too much time," Ms. Flores went on. "When we roll, you play as if it's the world championship. Volley until I say 'And go!' Then set it up so that Chad spikes one. When the ball hits the sand, the game is over. I want to see yelling, screaming, high-fives, hugs, the works. Then, instantly — break. You all start reapplying your Day-Nite sunscreen, which we're setting up on a blanket. Roxanne will be the center of the action, and . . . um, Abby, you bump into her. She yells in pain. Don gently presses a finger on her arm to show the burn. See, she's the one who doesn't use our product. And then, everyone, your puppy was just run over. Got it?"

Everybody nodded, and the two teams lined up again. " 'Your puppy was just run over'?" I whispered to Linda.

"It's an expression," she explained. "It's

what the old-time Hollywood directors used to say to child actors when they wanted them to cry on film. She means, look concerned and sad for Roxanne."

"That's horrible!" I said.

Linda shrugged. "That's show biz."

As we volleyed some more, I could see Claudia, Dawn, Mary Anne, Stacey, Jessi, Robert, Logan, and Mrs. Hall walking toward me. I waved to them.

"Are those your friends?" Roxanne asked.

"Yup." My brain started screaming, *Eighteen, Abigail, you're supposed to be eighteen!* "I mean, my . . . younger sister's friends. But that makes them my friends, too, I guess."

Before I could feel like too much of a fool, Ms. Flores shouted, "Okay, are we ready for take one? Start playing hard now."

Jim, who was on our side, served the ball. I bounced on my feet, ready for anything.

"And . . . rolling!" Ms. Flores called out.

This was it. The moment of truth. The camera was going.

"YEEEEAAAA, ABBY!" my friends were shouting.

The ball was flying in my direction, high and very close to the net. A perfect spike if I ever saw one. I ran toward it. I jumped as high as I could, fist tight.

"Yaaaaah!" I yelled, whacking the ball with all my strength.

It smashed over the net and bounced in the sand.

"Cut!" Ms. Flores yelled.

I looked around. Chad was laughing, and I had no idea why.

"Uh, Abby?" Ms. Flores said. "That's not in the script. Remember?"

She repeated her instructions. I felt like an idiot. "I'm sorry," I said about a thousand times.

"One more thing," Ms. Flores went on. "Enjoy yourself, okay? This isn't the Olympics."

"Okay."

As play started, I smiled. I laughed for no reason. I was going to have the time of my life if it killed me.

Ms. Flores yelled "Cut" when the ball went bouncing away. And again when a little boy went running through our team. And again when Don elbowed Chad in the face.

Roxanne had been made up to look as if she had a terrible sunburn. But when it came time for me to bump into her, I was the one who screamed.

Roxanne may have been the one without Day-Nite suntan lotion, but I was the one without any at all.

I checked my watch. It was already ten-thirty. I'd been in the sun for three hours. And we still weren't done.

During a break, I coated myself with Day-Nite sunscreen. It smelled awful.

Besides, at that point, I don't know how much good it could have done. I was already fried.

Oh, well, I guess it was a small price to pay.

No one ever said stardom was easy.

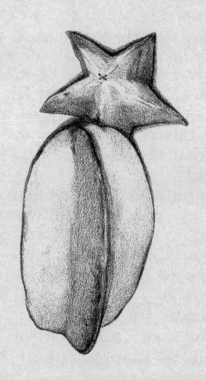

CHAPTER 11

Stacey

Friday

Wowee, Maui! I am flying over the island of Maui as I write this. In my guidebook, it says that Hawaiians call Maui no ka ŏi, which means "the best." I can see why. From the air, it's stunning. It looks like two rugged mountains that bumped into each other and decided to stay together as one island.

Kind of like Robert and me.

Just kidding! Anyway, we're going to stay here through the weekend and camp out on the slopes of a humongous volcano. On Sunday, we take a helicopter ride over the volcano.

Will I be caught in an eruption? Will I be blasted out of the sky?

Will I discover an ancient lava lamp?
I'll keep you posted.

"All I said was, 'Lookin' good,'" Robert pleaded. "She was offering us something to drink."

"I know, but it was the way you said it." I tried to imitate the way Robert was ogling the flight attendant and lowered my voice. "'Lookin' goooood.' I didn't know you liked brunettes."

"I was talking about the *juice*, Stacey, not the stewardess."

"Flight attendant. Don't be so sexist."

Robert burst out laughing. "Stacey, what has gotten into you? You're joking, right?"

I looked out the window. I hadn't been joking at all. But even as I was saying the words, I knew they didn't sound like me. I'm not usually the jealous type, yet I was so suspicious of Robert.

I know he's not a two-timer or a liar. That's not his nature. And on this trip he'd been nice and considerate and handsome and charming. All that good stuff.

The problem was, he'd been nice and considerate and handsome and charming to a lot of girls. Especially one particular girl on the flight from New York. Blonde, blue-eyed, pretty, slimy, disgusting Sue Archer.

"Stacey, why are you being so weird?" Robert asked. "Are you still mad about Sue? I told you I didn't mean anything serious — "

"You spent more time with her on the plane than with me!"

Robert put his arm around me. "That's because she wouldn't stop talking. Besides, I'm with you now, aren't I?"

I exhaled deeply. I didn't shake off his arm, but I also wasn't exactly cuddly.

Sue was a big talker. Robert was right. Maybe I should just lighten up, I thought. We were in the world's most romantic place. Why not just relax, snuggle with Robert, enjoy it all?

I started to lean back. But Robert was already pulling his arm away. He reached into the seat-back pouch in front of him and took out a magazine.

My head snuggled back against worn-out nylon plush.

Minutes later, we were descending into Maui's Kahului Airport. (The flight from Oahu to Maui is super-short.)

Mr. De Young, our chaperone, turned to face us from his seat across the aisle. "Everyone stick together. Let's get out of the airport as fast as possible. The trip to the crater takes almost two hours."

Stacey

Our group had only seven kids, including Robert and me, so we could move pretty fast. When the plane landed, we followed Mr. De Young into the terminal and claimed our packs. (We were camping out, so we'd each brought camping packs crammed with everything we needed — including heavy clothes, rain gear, and sleeping bags.)

At a rent-a-car counter, the clerk greeted us with a big smile. "I just called for weather conditions," he said. "Right now, Haleakalā is bright and sunny. But you never know. Upcountry, the weather can change in a minute. The crater gathers up all the trade winds and clouds, and it can be cold."

"Thanks," Mr. De Young said. "Can I rent a minivan with snow tires?"

After signing all the papers, Mr. De Young gave Robert a road map and appointed him navigator. We all went outside and piled in the van.

"Upcountry" meant the interior of Maui, where the highway rises up the side of Haleakalā. It's one of the steepest car rides in the world. We passed huge farms, cactus-filled plains, and patches of vivid flowers.

I sat in back with Pete Black and Mari Drabek, while up front Mr. De Young and Robert chatted about sports and road directions.

My stomach didn't do too well as the road

115

started turning sharply. But we took a break just in time, at the park headquarters. (The first thing I did was pull out my down jacket. It was *freezing*.) By this time it was already afternoon, and the rangers told us the volcano was covered with clouds.

"Bummer," Mr. De Young said.

"Not really," one of the rangers said. "It's a perfect day to see a Brocken specter."

"A what?" Robert asked.

The man winked. "Go to the Leleiwi Overlook and keep your eyes on the clouds."

We took his advice and parked at the overlook. Even overcast (or *undercast*, since we were so high up), the view from the volcano's edge was spectacular. Inside the valley of the big crater, smaller craters rose up through the cloud cover.

Then I heard Robert gasp. "Stacey, look!"

I gazed upward. There, hovering above the volcano against the fluffy gray-white clouds, was my silhouette. Over my head arched a brilliant rainbow.

"Awesome," muttered Mari.

"So this shadow is a Brocken specter," Mr. De Young said. "I wonder what it's supposed to mean?"

"Fame and fortune," Robert said.

"Seven years' bad luck," Pete Black chimed at the same time. (Nice guy, huh?)

We climbed back into the van and chugged farther up the foggy, wet road. At one point we passed a sign that said NENE CROSSING. The nene is the Hawaiian state bird, a type of goose without webbed feet. (We didn't actually see one cross the road, but I think I spotted one flying overhead.)

Finally, after a slow, twisting ride, we reached the top — Pu'u Ula'ula.

How can I describe the view? "Awesome" is too weak a word. The clouds had begun to burn off, and the valley stretched out before us, rolling into the distance and looking like the face of the moon.

We were all too thunderstruck to speak. Finally Robert stood next to me and put his arm around my shoulders. "The guidebook says that the entire island of Manhattan could fit in there."

I tried to picture it. I glanced over to what would be the Upper West Side. "Not a good idea," I said. "I wouldn't want to live in a crater. Besides, the subway would be too hot."

Robert lowered his arm. "I was only kidding."

Ugh. He looked offended. I hadn't meant my comment to be snide. "Well, so was I."

"Uh-huh." He nodded. I nodded.

We glanced out over the big, gaping hole.

CHAPTER 12

Claudia

Friday

Stacey, Robert, and a few other kids flu to mowy today. The rest of us ~~journy journie~~ went on a bus ride through the Coolaw mountans to windword Oahio, where our new hotell is.

We saw a clift where hunderds of soldgiers were pushed to there deaths in a war. To get that authentique feel, we had to take the jump ourselus.

Dont wurry, just jocking.

Any way, the day started with a trip to the very plesent sumer house of Queen Ema.

 W ell, it didn't actually start there. I left out our first stop. Punchbowl Crater National Memorial Cemetery of the Pacific.

It's a graveyard of soldiers — thirty thousand of them, mostly from the Vietnam War and World War Two. In the center, a long flight of stairs leads up to a monument to the dead.

Part of the monument is a long marble wall, etched with maps of famous battles. Including, of course, Pearl Harbor.

When I saw it, I felt a little sick. My visit to the *Arizona* memorial had been on my mind for two days. I'd awakened that morning with a horrible dream. In it, I was a Japanese spy in Pearl Harbor during the attack. I escaped harm, but then an American general took a look at me and realized I was one of the enemy. A whole batallion of soldiers started chasing me, as bombs exploded in the background and a Japanese plane swung by with a rope for me to grab onto.

I think I screamed myself awake. But Dawn and Mary Anne didn't hear me. They were still fast asleep.

Now, at Punchbowl, I was in no mood for reminders. I turned away quickly and headed down the steps.

"Where are you going?" asked Mary Anne.

"Back to the bus," I said. "This is interesting, but you know, time to move on . . ."

I felt so self-conscious. My face was burning. On my way down, I avoided looking at old people. What if they had been around back then, like Mr. Blanchard at the *Arizona* memorial? What if they were paying respects to one of their relatives or friends who was killed at Pearl Harbor? How could they possibly forgive the Japanese?

I picked up speed.

Out of the corner of my eye I saw a group of Japanese tourists walking upward, slowly and solemnly. Did they feel the same way I did? I thought about joining them, trying to lose myself in their midst.

But I didn't. At the bottom of the steps, I hung out by the entrance. I mingled with the eucalyptus trees until everyone came filing back. Then I slipped onto the bus and sat quietly next to Mary Anne.

She was eyeing me warily. "Tired?" she asked.

"Yup." I faked a yawn. "Wake me up when we get to the beach."

A few minutes later we pulled up to the place I mentioned in Mal's journal, the summer palace of a Hawaiian queen named Emma. Actually, *palace* was kind of a grand word for it. *Oversized, white-shingled New England cottage* was more like it. The house was cute, a little like some nice, normal Stoneybrook homes. At least on the outside.

The inside was a different story. Emma had the coolest taste — feather capes, huge paintings, intricate wall hangings, and textured fabrics I'd never seen before.

"I could live here," Mary Anne remarked.

"Nahh, not close enough to the water," Abby said.

Poor Abby. Her face was the color of a boiled lobster. The rest of her body must have been badly burned, too, because she was walking like the Tin Man.

"Maybe Queen Emma wasn't a surfer girl like you," Logan remarked.

" 'Dooooo youuuuu love me, dooo youuuu, suuurfer giiirl?' " sang Alan (the Goon) Gray.

A guide gave him a sharp Look. (So did Mr. Kingbridge.)

"Sorry." Alan weaseled away, pretending to be interested in the surroundings.

Mary Anne, Jessi, and I came across a dramatic picture of Emma's son, Prince Albert. "I guess this was way before, like, governors and mayors and stuff," I remarked.

"Huh?" Mary Anne looked at me blankly.

"I mean, states don't have kings and queens and princes anymore," I explained.

Jessi burst out laughing. "Hawaii wasn't always a state, Claudia. It used to be its own country."

Duh. Open mouth, insert foot.

"I knew that," I lied.

I could hear Alan snickering.

I decided to wander off and investigate Emma's backyard, where I might not be tempted to ask stupid questions.

Near the house was a basketball court. (I imagined a duke in high-tops calling inside, "Your Majesty, thy court is prepared!") Just beyond it I spotted a small, strange-looking white cottage. I walked closer and noticed an intricate rope hanging over the entrance.

A plaque in front identified it as a Shinto temple. Shinto is a Japanese religion. I remembered seeing buildings like this one in Mimi's old photos.

Weird. What was it doing here? Was Queen Emma Japanese? Did she have Japanese neighbors?

Either way, I'll bet Emma rolled over in her grave when she heard about the attack on Pearl Harbor.

Argggh. *That place* again. I just couldn't get away from it, no matter where I went on this island.

I walked back to the house. At the entrance, I stopped to let a group of tourists exit.

We exchanged polite hellos.

"Thank you, that was very interesting," one of them said to me.

"Oh, I don't work — " I began.

"Which is the correct pronunciation," blurted out a youngish guy in the group, "Ha-*wa*-ee or Ha-*va*-ee?"

"Um, well, I'm not Hawaiian. I'm — " My tongue froze in my mouth. My brain took me on a detour from the last word in that sentence.

I swallowed and said, "Asian."

"I think it's Ha-*va*-ee," an older guy in the group said.

"Thank you," said the first man.

"You're *velcome*!" answered the second.

Well, they thought that was the funniest thing ever said. They all walked away, laughing like hyenas.

I felt like crawling under the floorboards.

The rest of the trip? Fine, I guess. We took a gorgeous drive through the Ko'olau Mountain Range. On the way, we stopped at a famous place called Nu'uanu Pali Lookout, a sheer cliff with a breathtaking view of Windward Oahu.

We learned that good old King Kamehameha once drove hundreds, maybe thousands of enemy soldiers to their deaths over the edge of that cliff.

Senseless deaths.

Again. Like at you-know-where.

It was a recurring theme in Hawaii.

Who knows? Maybe the king was part Japanese, too.

CHAPTER 13

Mary Anne

Friday

Guess what we
can see from our
hotel?

Gilligan's Island!

I'm serious. You
know the stormy-
looking island they
show during the
theme song? That's
the one!

Abby thinks it's an
omen. She thinks it
means her acting career
is headed toward
sitcoms.

I hope she's right.
Then she'll make

125

MaryAnne

*enough money to
bring us all back
here again. . . .*

"It looks different," Jessi said, peering out at
the island in Kaneohe Bay.

"Well, the show *is* old," Abby remarked,
slathering her face with sunblock as thick as
Elmer's Glue. "Besides, the Skipper and Gilligan cut down a lot of the original trees to
build houses and stuff."

"I saw him, you know," Dawn said. "Gilligan. He was in a dinner theater show near
L.A. He's not young anymore."

Dawn, Abby, Jessi, Claudia, and I were
poolside at the SeaView Family Resort. It was
in a community called Kaneohe, on the windward side of Oahu, over the Ko'olau Mountains from Honolulu. (Don't let the name
Windward Oahu give you the wrong impres-
sion. It's not stormy and chilly. The wind is
gentle, warm, and fragrant.)

The resort wasn't exactly super-modern, but
it was huge — two swimming pools, a golf
course, and a restaurant. And I adored the
hotel managers, Mr. and Mrs. Reynolds. (Mrs.
Reynolds was the one who told us about Gilligan's Island, which is actually called Coconut
Island.) They're real Hawaiians. You can't tell

by their last name, but you can by their Polynesian looks. They both have dark, golden
skin and black hair.

When we asked if we could room together,
Mrs. Reynolds assigned Claudia and me to the
same room, and she put Abby, Dawn, and
Jessi in the next room.

Now, as the sun set behind us, we were
hanging out at one of the pools and enjoying
the view.

"Claudia, Kristy, and I used to watch that
show all the time," I said.

I looked over at Claudia, but she was gazing
off into the distance.

I was concerned about her. She hadn't
seemed herself the last few days. I'd asked her
what was wrong a hundred times. But she
always smiled and said everything was fine.

Well, it wasn't. I knew it. And I was determined to talk to her about it.

I had my chance when we went to our room
to prepare for dinner.

"Claudia, won't you tell me what's both-
ering you?"

Claudia started fumbling with the buttons
on her blouse. "Nothing. Why?"

"You've been so down. I thought you were
going to cry at Punchbowl Cemetery."

"Cry?" Fumble, fumble. "Me? Why would
I do that?"

A button came off in her hand. Claudia sat there, staring at it, turning it over and over.

I began changing out of my bathing suit. "Just asking."

Claudia took a deep breath. "Mary Anne, what ethnicity are you?"

Huh? I hadn't expected a question like that. I finished pulling on my clothes and sat next to Claud on the bed. "Well, a little German, a little Norwegian, some — "

"Have you ever felt, like, guilty for what the Germans did in World War Two?" she interrupted me.

"I hadn't thought about it." So *that's* what this was about. "Oh, Claudia, you're not still thinking about what we saw at Pearl Harbor!"

Claudia's head sank. "How could they have done that, Mary Anne? My ancestors! And everyone in Hawaii puts on such a friendly face. It's as if they've all forgotten about it."

"It was a long time ago, Claud."

"Yeah, but think of all the survivors. Not only buddies, like Mr. Blanchard's. But brothers and sisters of sailors who died. Sons and daughters. Little kids who never met their fathers. Wives who had to explain to their children that their daddies weren't coming home."

Oh boy. My eyes were starting to water. "Claudia, you can't take this so personally."

"You know, my parents always taught me to respect my elders. No one ever thought I took that seriously, but I always have. Mimi was my guardian angel. And now I can't even think of her the same way, Mary Anne. I mean, she was in Japan at the time. She was on the other side."

"Maybe she was against the attack. Maybe that was one of the reasons she came here," I suggested.

"Maybe," Claudia mumbled.

I put my arm around her and smiled. "Look, let's go have our dinner. I'm sure you'll feel better with a full stomach."

Claudia grumbled something and finished dressing.

We didn't say a word as we walked to the restaurant.

Well, Claudia slowly cheered up during dinner. By bedtime, she was talking excitedly about our scheduled tour of Windward Oahu the next day.

As we waited in the lobby on Saturday morning for our group to gather, a family with two girls was checking out at the front desk.

The littler girl, who looked about three, skipped over to us. "I have two Barbies," she announced.

Her older sister ran up beside her. "She

thinks Barneys are Barbies. She always makes that mistake."

"They're both very nice," I said. "What are your names?"

"I'm Nikki Harbison. I'm seven. Show them how old you are, Evie."

"This many." The littler girl struggled to hold up three fingers.

"Joseph is five," Nikki went on.

"Where's he?" I asked.

Nikki shrugged. "I don't know."

"Nikki, Evie, Joseph!" called the kids' mom. "Let's go!"

"Well, it was nice to meet you," Claudia said, standing up. " 'Bye."

" 'Bye!" the girls cried, skipping away.

"Where's Joseph?" I heard Mr. Harbison say.

"Wasn't he with you?" his wife answered.

"J-o-o-seph!" called Mr. Harbison, running off.

Mrs. Harbison left their luggage at the front desk and walked away in the other direction, holding her daughters' hands. "Joe?"

By now the lobby was full of SMS students. Mr. Kingbridge was scribbling something on an itinerary sheet.

But my attention was on Mrs. Reynolds. "Tell the kitchen staff to be on the lookout for a blond five-year-old boy," she said into the hotel phone. Then she hung up and called to a bellhop, "George, check the pools and have someone go to the game room."

When Mrs. Reynolds saw me watching, she signaled me over. "You were talking to the girls. Did they say anything about their brother?"

"No," I replied.

Mr. and Mrs. Harbison both returned to the desk. Without Joseph.

They seemed frantic. "We can't find him anywhere!" Mrs. Harbison said.

"Mommy, is Joseph lost?" Evie asked.

"Of course he is!" Nikki said.

"Ma'am, I'd be happy to look after the girls if you want to go search some more," Mrs. Reynolds said.

The two parents talked briefly. "Well, all right," Mrs. Harbison said. "Girls, you stay close to the nice lady."

I could see how busy Mrs. Reynolds was. She certainly didn't need two little girls running around the lobby. What if she had an emergency of her own?

I ran up to Mr. Kingbridge, explained the situation, and asked if I could stay.

"Well, I suppose so," he replied. "Mrs. Hall is staying behind. Just keep in touch with her."

"Thanks!" I replied.

I told Claudia what I was doing. She wished

131

me good luck as she filed out the front door with the group.

I ran to Mrs. Reynolds and told her I could help out.

"I'll stay with the girls right now," she said. "You check the hallways. Start from the top and work down."

The SeaView had three connected buildings. I took the elevator to the top of the one we were in and worked my way down. When I reached the bottom, Mrs. Reynolds was frantically signaling me. "Would you stay with the girls for a moment? One of the busboys says he thinks he saw a boy walking alone across the park."

She jogged out of the building. The girls were sitting in the lobby among their luggage. Nikki was reading a book and Evie was playing with numbered blocks.

"When are they going to find him?" Evie whined.

"Soon," I reassured her.

But I wasn't so sure. Mr. and Mrs. Harbison kept running in and out, looking more and more panicked. I introduced myself and they seemed to trust me instantly. (Maybe that was because they saw the word *Baby-sitters* on the BSC T-shirt I was wearing.)

Mrs. Reynolds came back half an hour later

with no news. We switched places, and I continued the search.

By now, practically the entire hotel staff was involved. The police had been called, too. A squad car was parked out front, and I could see an officer talking intently to Mr. Harbison.

I double-checked the Harbisons' old room, which was open. I found a seashell and a green plastic pail, but no little boy.

I was worried. It was eleven o'clock, and Joseph had been gone an hour and a half.

When I returned to the lobby, Evie was in tears. "A robber took him!" she was screaming. "And he drowneded him!"

"Shhh, shhh," Mrs. Reynolds was saying. "Let's make some numbers with your blocks."

My mind was racing. What if I were Joseph in this hotel? What would make me leave my family?

Seeing something cool. Needing to use the bathroom. Going back to my room to find something I'd forgotten . . .

I ruled all of those out. The lobby looked normal, the bathrooms had been checked, the room was empty.

Mrs. Reynolds was holding Evie in her lap and shuffling blocks. "Now, what was your room number?"

"Three . . . and four," Evie muttered.

"No, Evie," Nikki said. "It's *two four three!*"

Bing! It hit me. Maybe Joseph had wanted to go back to his room. But he was only five. What if he'd forgotten the number?

"I'll be right back!" I called out.

Two four three.

I took the elevator to the fourth floor. I tried Room 432 and 423. One was locked, the other open but empty.

Same with rooms 342 and 324 on the third floor — one locked, one empty.

I went downstairs and tried the door for room 234. It was locked, so I knocked once, twice.

No answer.

I felt as if all the air were rushing out of me. My body slumped as I walked to the elevator.

"Who is it?"

I almost didn't hear the little voice. I spun around and ran back to room 234.

"Joseph?" I called out.

"Uh-huh."

"Can you open up?"

"Are you a stranger?"

"My name is Mary Anne. I'm a friend of Evie and Nikki's. Can you open the door, please?"

"Uh-uh. It's stuck."

"Give it a good, hard turn, Joseph. The knob is kind of old-fashioned."

I could hear him grunting. With a loud click, the door opened.

A blond, brown-eyed, dimply boy smiled bashfully at me. "I really am strong."

I had to wipe my eyes dry. I took Joseph by the hand and led him down the hall. "Joseph, your mom and dad are so worried about you. What happened? Did you forget something?"

"My big shell. But you know what? That wasn't our room. I thought it was, but the toilet was on the wrong side. The door was open, but I closed it by mistake. And I couldn't get it open. And you know what?"

"What?"

"I didn't cry. Well, a little bit. Then I fell asleep on the big bed. Then you knocked on the door."

We rode the elevator down to the lobby. The moment the door opened, Mrs. Harbison let out a sort of half-scream, half-sob. She and her husband rushed to Joseph and scooped him up, kissing him, thanking me, hugging him, and scolding him all at the same time.

"Let *me* kiss him!" Evie cried out. She and Nikki were beaming.

"Good work," Mrs. Reynolds said, hanging up the hotel phone. "I just called the police to tell them what happened. How did you find him?"

I explained everything. The police came,

and I repeated it all to them. Mr. and Mrs. Harbison couldn't stop thanking me.

While the Harbisons were collecting themselves in the lobby, Mrs. Reynolds looked curiously at my T-shirt. "What's the Baby-sitters Club?"

"This group I belong to back home," I said. "We do a lot of sitting."

"How'd you like to pick up a job here?"

"Really?"

"Well, you seem pretty terrific with kids. My husband and I have three. Our regular daytime sitter is sick. My father-in-law lives with us, but he can't fill in tomorrow, because he'll be away. Would you be interested?"

Would I? Spending a day with a typical Hawaiian family? Learning about another culture firsthand?

"Sure I would," I replied. "But I'll have to check with one of our chaperones."

"What's the name?" Mrs. Reynolds asked. "I'll call from the switchboard, and you can ask."

You know what Mrs. Hall's response was? "You want to baby-sit on vacation?"

I thought about it, but my mind was made up. I said yes, and she gave me permission.

"It's okay," I told Mrs. Reynolds.

"What a relief," she said. "My husband will pick you up here tomorrow at nine o'clock."

CHAPTER 14

Dawn

Friday
One day, when I was
in L.A. with my dad, the
wind was blowing in from
the ocean, which it hardly
ever does. The sky was
absolutely clear. It was
such a shock to see unpol-
luted air in L.A. that people
were driving to the beach
just to stand and look at
the sky.

Hawaii's a different
story. Here, the air is always
fresh and the water perfect.
So when you see what I
saw today, it really throws
you....

"Come on, Dawn, it's not so bad!" Abby called out.

She, Logan, Claudia, and a couple of other kids raced each other into the water.

"Later," I shouted.

Honestly, I didn't have the urge.

I don't know what I was expecting. Maybe a pristine stretch of sand with a few palm trees and a ukelele band. Maybe another bustling resort beach with high-rises and surfers.

I sure wasn't expecting dark, brownish water with mudflats and a little strip of sand.

Okay, okay, I was spoiled, I admit it. But you try spending five days in paradise and see how you feel.

Jessi was sitting on the beach towel next to mine, talking into her tape recorder. "Hi, Mal. We're killing a few hours before lunch. Later, we're going to the North Shore of Oahu — "

I took the machine from her. "Hi, Mal!" I called into the built-in mike. "I'm going to ask Jessi if she wants to go in search of a better beach."

Jessi giggled and took it back. "Details later."

She snapped it off. We found Ms. Bernhardt and asked permission to wander away. She said fine, as long as we didn't go too far.

We set off, heading away from the SeaView.

What did we find? First a concrete dock with some boat launches. Then a grassy picnic area with a fried-fish shack.

"Let's go back," Jessi suggested.

A squealing group of children ran by, dressed in bathing suits. They scampered over a ridge at the other end of the field.

"Where are they heading?" I asked.

The kids had dropped out of sight, but we could hear them, laughing and splashing. We ran to the ridge and climbed over.

Then we stopped in our tracks.

It was a beach, all right. It had sand and palm trees and water. But it looked as though no one had cleaned it in years.

A broken cooler lay open a few feet away, with empty cans scattered around it. Old, torn clothing was draped over a shredded truck tire. A newspaper flew across the sand, wrapping itself around the trunk of a tree. Seagulls picked among the remains of an abandoned lunch.

The kids were swimming around, ignoring the bottles and wooden planks that bobbed in the water nearby.

I looked around for a trash can, but not one was in sight.

In the middle of the beach was an old wooden sign. We had to move close to read the faded print:

LOT FOR SALE
JL5-7289
SWIM AT YOUR OWN RISK!

"Yuck," Jessi remarked.

"How could people do this?" I said. "I mean, this could be a nice beach."

Jessi picked up a rent-a-car brochure. "Maybe it was. It looks as though lots of people came."

"And didn't clean up."

"Maybe the maintenance staff and lifeguards are on vacation."

"What maintenance staff? The sign says swim at your own risk. This isn't a public beach."

"It's private?"

"Well, I don't see a house nearby. But that sign says someone's trying to sell the land." I shrugged. "I don't know what you'd call it."

I spotted some broken glass by the ridge. I scooped up the pieces, dumped them in the cooler, and picked it up from the bottom. "I saw a Dumpster by the food shack," I said. "I don't want the kids to step on this glass."

"Ew! Get that away from me!" screamed one of the kids.

A boy was chasing after her with a seaweed-encrusted, waterlogged Raggedy Ann doll.

Jessi and I looked at each other. Then we

headed back over the ridge. I tossed the cooler into the Dumpster.

When we returned to the muddy beach, Jessi went right to her tape recorder and spiral notebook. Ms. Bernhardt was deeply into a thick book about Hawaii.

"It says here," she announced, "that Hawaii is the healthiest state in the country to live in. The average lifespan is the longest, because people just stay healthier in this climate and lifestyle." She put the book down and let out a whoop of laughter. "But tooth decay is thirty percent *above* the national average. Well, isn't that a hoot. Closet candy eaters. I suppose we all have our dirty little secrets, don't we?"

Wasn't that the truth. Like a certain beach just up the road.

A cavity. That's what it was like. A little area of decay in a beautiful mouth.

I had to do something about it. But what?

ROBERT

RIDE 'EM, PANIOLOS!

HEY, MALLORY. IT'S ME, ROBERT. I HOPE YOU DON'T MIND ME WRITING IN YOUR BOOK. STACEY SAID SHE'D TORTURE ME IF I DIDN'T. (HA HA, JUST JOKING.)

ANYWAY, WHEN YOU COME HERE SOMEDAY, DEFINITELY SWING OVER TO HALEAKALĀ NATIONAL PARK. (IF YOU START PRACTICING THE PRONUNCIATION NOW, YOU MAY GET IT BEFORE YOU LEAVE.) AND WHATEVER YOU DO, DON'T MISS GOING TO PANIOLO COUNTRY.

WE STOPPED FOR A LOOK ON OUR WAY DOWN FROM THE CRATER. AND I HAVE FINALLY SEEN WHAT I WANT TO DO FOR A LIVING....

"You're crazy," Stacey said.

"Am not," I replied. "Look at these dudes. They're cool."

Paniolos, in case you don't know, are Hawaiian cowboys. What a concept. Ride horses all day, rope steer, then grab a surfboard and head to the beach.

That, in my opinion, is the life.

Stacey didn't agree with me. "Robert, you can't just *be* one. First of all, they're Hawaiian. Second of all, they're . . . never mind."

"They're what?"

"Well . . . tough."

"Hey —"

"I mean, outdoors tough. Not sports tough. You know what I mean."

"I do?"

"*Robert!*"

I was trying. Joking, smiling, being as nice as I could. But Stacey was like a broken faucet. I couldn't tell whether she was going to be warm or cold.

She was still jealous that I had been talking with Sue Archer, back on the flight from New York. Well, I like Sue, okay? I mean, not *like* like. I *like* like Stacey. It's completely different.

Or maybe it isn't. I'm kind of messed up about it, I guess.

All I know is that I'd had the coolest twenty-four hours of my whole life, and I'd spent it with Stacey, and half the time she wanted to be on a different planet from me.

The other half, she was her funny, smiling self.

On Friday, we stayed up on Haleakalā until sunset. That killed me. The sun was so huge I thought it had fallen right through the atmosphere.

Afterward we ran back to the minivan, because Mr. De Young was scared to drive down those hairpin turns in the dark. We only had to go as far as the campgrounds, though. He'd brought a couple of lightweight tents, so we split up, boys/girls, and pitched camp for the night.

It was pretty cold, but we all had down sleeping bags. I woke up while it was still dark, feeling great. Stacey complained about her hair.

We convinced Mr. De Young to drive to the top and watch the sunrise. Would you believe we hit a traffic jam on the way up? I saw why when we arrived. The sunrise was even more spectacular than the sunset.

Then we took a hike into the crater. I nearly jumped out of my hiking boots when I saw a boar running across the path. And I pretended to jump into the Bottomless Pit, this hole where early Hawaiians used to throw their babies' umbilical cords (hey, I don't understand it, either).

Stacey's favorite part was seeing silversword plants. They're huge, spiny things that take ten or twenty years to grow, bloom once, then die. Pretty grim life, if you ask me.

After the hike we piled into the van and drove to a botanical garden, where Stacey bought a protea flower (which looks like a Koosh ball) to press and put in Mal's scrapbook. That was kind of fun, but nothing like the *paniolos*. They were farther down the road, where the land flattens out.

We watched the old cowpokes for awhile, and then Mr. De Young gave us the signal to leave.

"So long, guys!" I called out.

One of them actually waved to me.

"Robert, don't embarrass me," Stacey said, ducking into the minivan.

As we drove on, we passed a huge field of brilliant red flowers. "Poppies!" exclaimed Renee Johnson.

"Scarecrow, I feel tired," I said, leaning my head on Stacey's shoulder.

"Oh, thanks," Stacey snapped. "Are you saying my hair makes me look like a scarecrow? How sweet."

"No! It was a joke. You know, like Dorothy falling asleep in *The Wizard of Oz*? In the poppy field?"

"You don't look like Dorothy," Pete Black said in his most obnoxious voice.

"At least I'm not a cowardly lion," I shot back.

"*Guys . . .* " Mr. De Young warned us from the front seat.

"Can I get out and hitchhike?" Stacey asked.

After awhile we passed a field of long, stiff shoots, waving in the breeze. "What's that stuff?" I asked.

"Sugarcane," Mr. De Young explained.

Stacey sneered (she's diabetic). "Ugh."

Well, it goes to show you how stupid I am. I thought sugar was dug out of mines.

Don't worry. I didn't say a word. I do have my pride.

That night we stayed in Kahului, then woke up Sunday morning and drove right to the helicopter company.

This was the part of the tour I'd been looking forward to the most. Stacey was psyched, too.

A chopper was revving up as our guide came to greet us. He had to shout to be heard. *"Welcome! I'm Jim Fredericks and I run this place! Only four passengers fit in each helicopter, so I've reserved two of them for you! Follow me!"*

146

He led us onto the field and started shouting directions — don't stand in the chopper, use the barf bags if necessary, stuff like that.

Stacey squeezed my hand. That felt great.

"Now," Mr. Fredericks yelled. *"I'll take you four . . ."*

He gently pushed Pete Black toward the helicopter, then Renee, then Mari.

Then his hand landed on Stacey's shoulder. She let go of my hand and gave me a helpless look.

I followed her to the chopper. "Uh, wait, uh, can we — " I said.

"Sorry, only four!" Mr. Fredericks bellowed. *"Plenty of room in the other one!"*

"But — but we — "

It was no use. My voice was swallowed up by the noise of the rotor blades.

"Don't worry," Mr. De Young said with a smile. "You can wave to each other across the volcano. Very romantic."

I punched him in the shoulder. He laughed.

Oh, well, it was only going to be a short trip. I could deal with it.

Stacey

Sunday

Guess where I am, Mal?
Give up? In a helicopter!

It's my first time. It is sooooooo amazing. I feel like an eagle. A very loud eagle. You wouldn't believe the noise.

Well, I thought Haleakalā was stunning from the top of the crater. From the air it takes my breath away . . . .

"To your right is the Bubble Cave," Mr. Fredericks announced, "where the bubbling molten lava cooled and hardened."

We swooped downward. My stomach jumped. Pete Black looked about ready to pass out.

I put down my spiral notebook, which calmed my stomach. I could see Robert's helicopter veering off in another direction. I felt a kind of tug inside. Despite all our arguing, I guess I still cared about him.

But, to be honest, I wasn't thinking too much about him. At least not for the moment. I was thinking about my life.

I cherished it. And up in a helicopter, I was realizing how fragile it was.

I mean, imagine being in a small car hurtling through the air. That's what it felt like. Not exactly cozy and safe.

"The bubbles you see now are not lava formations," Mr. Fredericks announced as we swung in another direction. "They're the domes of Science City, an observatory and research center. Let's give 'em a wave — they might be looking at us through their telescopes!"

Mari and Renee waved. Pete Black made a goon face. (Somehow I could not deal with dumb jokes at a time like this.)

As the helicopter turned around, I gasped. Dark clouds were tumbling over the far edge of the crater.

"As you can see, the weather can change in a minute upcountry," Mr. Fredericks said cheerfully. "Let's swing out over the lip and take a gander at the forest."

I couldn't believe it. He was heading *into* the storm. "Isn't this . . . dangerous?" I asked.

"Not at all," Mr. Fredericks replied with a chuckle. "The crater contains the clouds. Over the edge, we'll be leeward, in dry country. Besides, these choppers fly in any kind of weather condition. I figure we'll just beat the moving front . . ."

The clouds were racing toward us, swallowing up the cinder cones and rock formations. Half of the crater seemed to have disappeared.

Now, in my opinion, it would make sense to turn the other way. But no. Mr. Fredericks was heading to our right, to the edge of the crater. Right *into* the edge of the crater. I could practically count the rocks.

My throat was suddenly parched. My knuckles were white from gripping the armrests. I could see sweat trickling down Mari Drabek's forehead. Pete was now turning a shade of green.

I didn't know which would hit us first. The storm or the crater's edge.

"Um . . . um," I stuttered.

Mr. Fredericks looked as if he were taking a slow, leisurely drive along the Ohio Freeway. "And after we check out what we call the 'dryland forest,' we'll head over to Iao Valley . . ."

We jerked upward. The crater's edge began to fall away. I could see Mr. Fredericks's eyes darting to the left nervously.

"There we'll see, uh, some interesting rock formations," he said, "including — now, hang on, we're going to hit a rough patch — including one that resembles the profile of, um, former President John F. Kennedy — okay, this'll feel a little bumpy here — um, I suppose you're too young to know who he was . . ."

Be quiet! I wanted to scream. We were higher than the edge of the crater now. We could see to the other side. Dry country, where the storm wasn't supposed to go.

But it was going there. I could see the clouds swirling over the top of the crater, like an explosion. Trees under it were bending in the wind.

Mr. Fredericks had seen it, too.

"Oh boy oh boy," he muttered, grabbing his two-way radio mike. "Headquarters, this is five oh one. We may have a wind shear. Do you read me?"

That was it for Pete. He bent forward and puked his breakfast into a bag.

"We're located at approximately — "

He didn't have a chance to finish.

The cloud hit. I could feel it in my teeth. We lurched to the right, as if we'd been smacked by a giant baseball bat. My seat belt pulled taut against my stomach. I fell against Renee, who was now screaming her brains out.

Or maybe that was me. I couldn't tell.

The chopper's engine was groaning. The blades sounded as if they were cutting through mud. The wind howled and rain slapped against the windows. Mr. Fredericks was yelling into the mike.

Now we were all shrieking. Clutching at one another.

And then we plunged. Straight down.

I couldn't breathe. The cries were trapped in my throat. My stomach could feel the drop, but my eyes saw only wet darkness.

Suddenly we broke through the clouds and I saw the tops of trees. Lot of trees. Spiraling under us, growing closer, like moving cork-screws.

I was dizzy. I was trying to scream. I was

thinking of my dad and mom, my friends, Robert . . .

And then I blacked out.

Smell was the first sense that returned to me. Pete Black's . . . accident seeped into my nostrils, shocking me back to consciousness.

What a rude awakening. I absolutely *hate* barf.

My eyes flickered open and I tried to move. My legs were jammed between an armrest and a door. Below me was a smooth, concave pane of glass. Unbroken, fortunately.

Slowly the memories were seeping into my brain. The storm. The plunge.

I'm alive. The words wiped out every other thought. I was still in the helicopter, and it was on its side.

I looked around. No one else was with me, not Mr. Fredericks, not any of my friends.

I swallowed hard. Had they fallen out? Was I really alone? Where was I?

And where was my pack, which contained my insulin? That was nowhere in sight, either.

From what little I could see, the sun was dappling the forest floor around me. It was as if the storm had never happened. Birds were screeching and cawing.

And among those sounds, I thought I could hear voices.

I twisted around and tried to move the seat that had pinned my lower body. It gave a little, and I slowly pulled out my legs.

"Okay, Stacey's next," Mr. Fredericks's voice said.

"I'm here!" I shouted.

His face peered through the pilot's door, which was above me, where the roof should have been. "Are you okay?" he asked. "Can you move?"

"Fine," I replied. "How about my friends?"

"A little shaken up, but okay."

I looked around frantically. "How about my pack?"

"That's out here, too, safe and sound."

Mr. Fredericks reached inside. I unbuckled my seat belt, grabbed his hand, and climbed out. The helicopter had landed against the side of a boulder, and I stepped onto that and hopped down.

"We actually made a decent landing," Mr. Fredericks said. "Unfortunately, I didn't clear the rock, so it pushed us over. Can you walk?"

I took a few painless steps. Mari, Pete, and Renee were standing a few feet away. They all looked grim, pale, and dirty.

"Morning." Pete forced a smile. "I trust your flight was comfortable?"

Only then did I realize how tense I was.

Because the tension came welling up from inside, and it exploded out in a huge fit of laughter.

Mari and Renee lost their somber expressions. They began to giggle. Then the giggles grew, until we were all doubled over, cackling hysterically with shock, relief, and sheer happiness at being alive.

Pete stood there, looking slightly confused. I think visions of the Comedy Store were forming in his brain.

CHAPTER 17

Mallory ☺

Sunday

Today I had to sit for Margo and Claire. Whew. They were hard to handle. Bouncing off the walls. Plus it was so muggy and miserable. I figured I'd take them to the park, so they could run under the sprinkler. They were thrilled....

"**S**prinkler?" asked Claire. "Why?"

"It's not that hot," Margo added.

"It'll be fun," I said.

"But we're having fun *here*," Claire insisted.

Okay, I was stretching the truth in my BSC notebook entry.

My sisters were as peaceful as can be. They were running around, playing tag in the yard. Also, it was actually pretty mild outside. But I was determined to go to that playground. I had some unfinished business there.

Margaret Wellfleet.

Ever since she'd called the BSC, I'd been thinking about her. Rerunning that day in my mind. Thinking of the things I should have said when she yelled at me.

In all my mental reruns, I always said the right things. I told her off. I recited every word that Kristy had said to me. And she shrank away, apologizing. Promising to give the BSC number to all her friends.

The horrible Tuesday had been five days ago, and I had not spotted old Margaret Wellfleet once. I'd been trying. In fact, I'd gone to that playground every day, sometimes with baby-sitting charges, sometimes alone.

I know, I know. Stalking people in playgrounds is not exactly a normal thing for an eleven-year-old girl to do. But I had to see her.

I had to show her I had a mind of my own. I wasn't the weak, incompetent, lazy kid she thought I was.

I was beginning to think she was a figment of my imagination.

"Put on your bathing suits," I said.

"Do we *have* to?" Claire whined.

"It'll be fun," I repeated. "Go."

Grumbling, my sisters went inside to change.

I felt a little guilty dragging them along on my quest. But I knew they'd have a good time.

(Margo, by the way, is seven and Claire's five. I also have an eight-year-old brother, Nicky; a nine-year-old sister, Vanessa; and ten-year-old triplet brothers, Byron, Jordan, and Adam.)

I rounded up some sand toys, and we left the house together.

As we approached the park, I kept my eyes peeled. I didn't recall exactly what Margaret Wellfleet looked like. I'd kind of blocked out her face. But I remembered some details: medium height, brownish hair, somewhere around my mom's age.

Which narrowed it down to about ninety percent of the adults in the park.

"Push me, push me!" Claire shouted.

She ran to the swings and hoisted herself on. I pushed her for awhile. I tried to teach her to pump. Later on I left her and helped Margo make a damp sand castle (I was the Royal Water Fetcher).

It was during one of my water runs that I saw HER. At the other end of the playground.

Margaret Wellfleet was sitting on a park bench, reading a magazine.

All the words, every sentence I'd practiced since Tuesday, swam around in my head. I thought about the friendly approach, sitting down and reintroducing myself. I thought about the direct approach, just hashing it out, not letting her get a word in edgewise.

I also had a water bucket in my right hand. (Heh heh.)

What did I do? None of the above. I just couldn't bring myself to confront her. The bucket was heavy. My other hand was shaking with nervousness. Queen Margo of Sand was waiting.

I hurried toward the castle.

A little boy, who looked around three years old, was walking away from Margo with one of her plastic shovels.

"Hey!" Margo yelled. "I'm using that!"

She ran over to him and held out her hand. "That's mine. Would you please give it to me?"

"Mine!" the boy said, stalking away.

I thought Margo might make a scene, but

she didn't. She stewed for a minute, then turned back to her castle, keeping an eye on the boy.

I dumped my water and started making wet sand blocks. The boy dug for a few moments, then wandered away from the shovel.

Margo was ready. She scampered over and took it back.

I gave her a wink. "Good move."

"More water, peasant!" Margo demanded.

I ran off with the pail. When I returned, the boy was standing next to Margo. Shrieking. *"I WANT THAT!"*

"Here," Margo said, handing him a smaller shovel. "Want to help?"

"NO! THAT'S A BABY SHOVEL! I WANT THE BIG ONE!"

"Sorry, I'm using it," Margo said stubbornly.

The boy began stamping his feet, kicking sand all over the place. *"GIVE IT TO ME GIVE IT TO ME!"*

My good BSC instincts were clicking in. I figured I'd let him pour the water. Get him involved in some fun aspect of castle-building. Distract him.

But I didn't have a chance. His mom swooped over from the other side of the park. "Colin, this is *not* acceptable behavior!" she scolded.

"YOU'RE *NOT UPSEPTABLE!*" Colin screamed.

"Don't you dare talk to Mommy like that! Bad boys talk like that!"

She yanked Colin away. His face was bright red. His little body was going wild, kicking and screaming.

And my jaw was scraping the ground.

Guess who Colin's mommy was? Margaret Wellfleet.

I wanted to laugh. I also wanted to cry. I felt bad for Colin. If she'd left him alone, I'm sure we could have calmed him down.

Now he was becoming worse and worse. He'd broken loose from his mom and was running away, screaming, "I HATE YOU! DO YOU HEAR ME, I HATE YOU!"

Boy, did those words sound familiar.

A girl, who seemed about five or six, was now standing over him with her arms folded. "You're a baby, Colin."

"Isabella, you leave him alone!" Margaret Wellfleet commanded.

Isabella was the spitting image of Colin. Except her face wasn't twisted with rage.

This was amazing. Good old Margaret Wellfleet had two kids!

"*WAAAAAAHHHH! THIS IS A STUPID PLAYGROUND!*"

Colin's tantrum made Jenny P.'s look mild.

He was throwing sand, rubbing it in his hair, smacking the slide as hard as he could.

"Colin James Wellfleet!" his mom said through clenched teeth. "You stop that at once!"

By now, lots of people were watching. And reacting. One mom scooped her daughter away from the flying sand.

Margaret Wellfleet was frantic. Her son was out of control.

And all she could do was leave him alone.

Let it boil over.

I tried not to grin. I raised my chin high. My task was simple. Look her straight in the eye and say, "Now, *what* was the best way to deal with a tantrum?"

Nahh, maybe just stick out my tongue.

I stood up. I took a few steps in her direction. I had the words prepared, even the tone of voice.

Then I stopped dead in my tracks.

I couldn't do it. I just couldn't be that mean.

Margaret Wellfleet looked totally helpless.

I slowly backed away.

Her eyes met mine briefly. They darted away, then came back. She had recognized me. I could tell.

She sort of glowered, as if I were intruding. But boy, did she look guilty. Her face was turning beet red.

"YOU'RE A BAD BAD BAD BAD MOMMY!" Colin screamed.

I didn't say a word.

Instead, I held her glance for a long moment. Then I turned away and walked calmly back to my sister.

I felt about ten feet tall.

CHAPTER 18

Mary Anne

Sunday

I feel like such a
dunce.

I couldn't wait to go
to the Reynoldses'. I
thought it would
be really interesting
to experience a different
culture. See Hawii from
the inside of a typical
home.

It was much, much
different than I
expected ...

Mary Anne

A*loha kakahiaka . . . Aloha kakahiaka . . .*

I recited the Hawaiian words for "Good morning" in my head over and over. In preparation for my job, I'd studied a whole bunch of phrases.

Unfortunately, I am not exactly a genius in languages. A lot of those phrases sounded the same to me.

When Mr. Reynolds walked in through the front door of the hotel, I stood up eagerly.

"Hello, Mary Anne!" he said.

"Aloha kalīkimaka!" I blurted out.

He looked at me blankly. "Merry Christmas to you, too."

I must have turned bright red. "I meant — "

He roared with laughter. "I know what you meant. It was a very good try. Come on out."

He held open the front door and gestured toward a minivan parked in front. "You know, my wife and I really appreciate your doing this on your vacation."

"I'm happy to do it," I said. "I've been wanting to meet . . . your family."

I almost said "a typical Hawaiian family." But I stopped myself. That sounded terrible. I mean, what if someone were visiting me in Stoneybrook and said, "I've been wanting to meet a typical suburban white family"?

I'd been doing some reading about Hawaii-

MaryAnne

ans. No one knows exactly where the first inhabitants came from. They may have sailed from Polynesia or the Asian continent. Nowadays they're only eleven percent of Oahu's population. So I was going to have a glimpse into a rare and wonderful part of American culture.

I still wondered about the name Reynolds. It seemed so un-Hawaiian. Maybe Mr. Reynolds had changed it from something else (although I didn't dare ask him).

Mr. Reynolds was dressed in shorts, flip-flops, and a bright shirt that looked hand-painted, with a huge map of Oahu on it.

He must have noticed that I was looking at it, because he said, "Like it? I use it for directions sometimes when I get lost."

He burst out laughing again, and I felt immediately at ease. We chatted all the way to his house, which was just up the coast from the SeaView.

We pulled up in front of a white-shingled ranch surrounded by gorgeous tropical flowers. Mrs. Reynolds met us at the door, wearing a colorful, flowing *muumuu*.

"Hi, come on in!" She turned and called into the house, "Scott! Lani! Come meet Mary Anne!"

As I walked into the front hallway, a boy and girl came bouncing in. He was wearing a

167

tank top with an I Love NY logo, baggy shorts, and Reeboks. She was dressed in a Disneyland T-shirt, cut-off jeans, and tennis shoes.

"Hi," they said.

"Scott's eight and Lani's five," Mrs. Reynolds said. "Come meet baby Raymond."

As we walked into the living room, Scott and Lani raced back into the kitchen and started wolfing down Apple Jacks and Cheerios.

Little Raymond was in a playpen, holding onto the side and bouncing up and down. An unwatched TV was blaring away nearby, and toys and games were strewn all over the carpeting and furniture. Everything seemed cozy and comfy and very . . . familiar.

I felt kind of deflated.

I don't know what I was expecting. Ukelele music floating through a thatched hut? Kids wearing grass skirts and *leis*? A *luau* for breakfast?

Okay, maybe not. But something a little different.

If it weren't for the tropical flowers and trees outside, I might have been in Stoneybrook.

"Deeeeesss!" said Raymond, pointing at me.

" '*This*' was one of his first words," Mrs. Reynolds explained. "By the way, he's already had breakfast. When Scotty and Lani are done, you can hang out here or take them to the park. You'll find some hot dogs and buns in the fridge for lunch, and I'll be home around three."

"My father may be home before either of us," Mr. Reynolds said. "That's what he looks like." He pointed to a framed photo on the wall. In it, a white-haired Caucasian man was hugging Scott and Lani.

"That's your dad?" I asked.

Mr. Reynolds laughed. "Yeah, I know, everyone says that. If it weren't for my mom, I'd think I was adopted."

I wanted to shrink away. I couldn't believe I'd made such a stupid remark.

From an end table, Mr. Reynolds picked up an old black-and-white wedding photo that showed a smiling blond G.I., arm-in-arm with a stunning young Hawaiian-looking woman. "They were married after the war. Mom died last year, and Dad moved in with us. Anyway, he's spending the weekend in L.A., at a re-union of his World War Two pals."

"His flight back is scheduled for this after-noon," Mrs. Reynolds explained. "But we've told him all about you. Anyhow, call us at the hotel if you have any questions, Mary Anne. And thanks again."

We exchanged good-byes, and they left.

"Deeess! Deeeess!" Raymond kept saying.

"That means he wants to be picked up," Scott called from the kitchen.

I lifted Raymond and he gave me a big hug.

"What a friendly boy," I remarked.

"Want to see what we have?" Scott blurted out.

"Sure," I replied.

He and Lani disappeared, then returned with two pairs of brand-new in-line skates.

"Wow," I said. "Cool."

"Toool," Raymond echoed.

"We know how to use them, too," Lani said. "Can you take us to the park?"

"You bet," I said.

I'd been away from baby-sitting for over a week, but my skills weren't too rusty. I checked Raymond's diaper, which was dry. I carried him to his nursery, found a diaper bag, and stuffed it with emergency supplies. Then I went to the kitchen and packed some snacks.

Scott and Lani were waiting outside, all decked out in their skates, helmets, and protective padding. I put Raymond in a stroller and followed the two older kids to the park.

I watched them zoom around. I played with Raymond on the grass. I gave them a snack. We were having so much fun we didn't arrive home until two.

Hot dogs, Kool-Aid, and ice cream cones were on the menu for lunch (baby food, too).

Then I put Raymond down for a nap and straightened up the house a bit. When Mr. and Mrs. Reynolds arrived home, I was playing video games with Scott and Lani.

"The place looks so neat!" Mrs. Reynolds exclaimed. "Mary Anne, you're a wonder. What are you doing tomorrow?"

"Uh, well, I'm not sure," I said. "Why?"

Mr. Reynolds sighed. "My dad called the hotel to say he's staying in L.A. an extra day."

"And our sitter's still sick," Mrs. Reynolds added, "although she insists she'll be all right by Tuesday. Now, I know this is asking a lot, but we sure could use your help another day. Just till my father-in-law comes home."

I felt kind of trapped.

I mean, I'd enjoyed myself. I liked the Reynoldses a lot. But to be honest, one day was enough.

I *was* on vacation, after all.

"Grandpa's not coming home today?" Lani asked.

"No, sweetie," her mom replied.

"Rats, I miss him."

I glanced over at the two photos of Mr. Reynolds's dad. A couple of glass-encased military medals stood next to the wedding picture, and above it was a citation for bravery from President Harry S. Truman. It would be fun to meet him. He probably had all kinds of interesting stories to tell about the war and about old Hawaii.

Then an idea popped into my head. Claudia should sit for the Reynoldses. It might improve her frame of mind. Besides, she'd mentioned she was running out of money.

"Well, I may want to stick with the tour tomorrow," I said to Mrs. Reynolds. "But if I do, maybe my friend Claudia could sit. She's a fantastic sitter. She's another member of the Baby-sitters Club."

"Perfect!"

Mrs. Reynolds thanked me a million times, and the kids hugged me good-bye.

I rode back to the hotel with Mr. Reynolds.

The lobby was crowded with SMS kids when we arrived. They were gathered around the front desk in a tight circle. In the middle of them, Mr. Kingbridge was talking on the phone. Ms. Bernhardt stood next to him, looking grim.

The place was silent, except for Mr. Kingbridge's voice.

"What do you mean, lost?" he shouted. "Where? What about the others? Are they all right?"

I ran up to Claudia and Dawn. "What happened?"

I hadn't seen Claudia look so upset since her grandmother died. "It's Stacey," she said, her voice wavering. "Her helicopter went down in a forest."

The words hit me like a sledgehammer. "Robert, too?" I asked.

Dawn shook her head. "He was in another helicopter, and he's fine. But he saw Stacey's helicopter disappear into a big storm."

My knees gave out. I sank into a chair and burst into tears.

CHAPTER 19

Claudia

Sunday

It's elven oclock at nite. Still havin't herd from Stacey. The serch partys were out looking all day, but they were calld off because of darkness.

Now noboddys' looking for Stacey. But we beleave shes still alive. Were staying up late. Manely becuz we cant sleep, but also out of ~~soliderit~~ ~~solebdar~~ togetherness.

We know shes alright. She just has to be....

"The storm came in high and fast," said the helicopter pilot on the ten o'clock news. "I turned away from it, but I guess Jim thought he'd duck over the lip of the crater."

"There's Robert," Jessi said.

Sure enough, Robert and two other kids were visible behind the pilot on the TV screen. They were all standing on a sunny landing field.

The sight of Robert's face made my heart sink. He looked awful, as if he'd been crying for hours.

Mary Anne, who really had been crying for hours, started up again.

The image faded, and a local news anchor appeared. "Rescue workers combed Haleakalā National Park, the Waihoi and Kipahulu valleys, and much of the dry-land forest. They will start again tomorrow morning at sunrise . . ."

Abby flicked off the TV. "Knowing Stacey, she's probably found the only electrical outlet in the forest."

"Maybe the rescuers should just listen for the sound of a hair dryer," I said.

Jessi smiled. "She could use the dryer to scare away the Death Marchers."

"The *who*?" Abby asked.

Jessi pulled her spiral notebook out of her

pack and leafed through it. "Let's see . . . the *Huaka'i o-po*. Death Marchers. I read about this. They're ghosts who march around with torches, but only from about seven-thirty to two in the morning, and if you see them, you . . ." Jessi's voice trailed off, and she closed the book.

"You what?" I asked.

"Well . . . die, but it's, you know, only a story."

"Lovely," Abby murmured. "Just what we need to hear."

We sat there for awhile, trying not to look too awkward. "Well, I know they'll find her tomorrow," I said.

"Yeah . . ."

"Sure . . ."

"Uh-huh . . ."

Everyone nodded. Everyone agreed. No one wanted to admit the truth.

We were all scared out of our minds.

"So!" Abby blurted out. "What are we all doing tomorrow, after we celebrate the big rescue?"

"I was going to go with Mr. Wong's group, to visit some famous Japanese temple," Jessi said.

"Ms. Bernhardt's checking out some of the beaches south of here," Abby added.

"Cool," Mary Anne remarked.

"Sounds like fun," Dawn said.

This conversation was getting to me. Talking about Stacey made me nervous enough — but trying not to talk about her was even worse!

I flopped down on my bed. "I'm beat. I'm going to bed."

Abby, Dawn, and Jessi all muttered in agreement. We said good night, and they shuffled off to their room.

Mary Anne and I headed for the bathroom. As I was brushing my teeth, she asked, "Um, Claudia, I was wondering what *your* plans are. Did you want to go to that temple?"

"Uh-uh. Ah wah to shoofooway — " I spat. "I want to stay far away from Japanese stuff on this trip. It reminds me of you-know-what."

"Uh-huh. Well, you know, I had a great time at the Reynoldses' today. The thing is, they asked if I could sit again tomorrow, but I think one day's enough."

"Can't they find someone else?"

"Well, I thought maybe you. You told me you needed the money, and they're such nice people."

"I don't know, Mary Anne," I said. "Baby-sitting in Hawaii?"

"It's only half a day. And you'll like them. You would really get a lot out of this job."

"Mary Anne, I *have* baby-sat for nice families before."

"But not as . . . interesting as this."

I wanted to laugh. Meek little Mary Anne was sounding like Kristy the steamroller.

But she had a point. I did need the money. And when I thought about the upcoming day, the other options weren't so great.

Mr. Kingbridge had said we were going ahead with all plans. He thought it would be healthier than sitting together at the hotel worrying.

Which only meant we'd be traveling around the island together worrying. I wasn't looking forward to that.

I had faith that Stacey would be found. All the news reports had said that the pilot was the best. He knew every inch of Maui and had never had an accident.

If I had to spend Monday morning waiting to hear about Stacey, why not baby-sit? I'd be away from the nervous atmosphere. And with three kids to care for, I wouldn't have time to worry.

"Okay," I said.

I had a hard time sleeping that night. I woke up before Mary Anne did and flicked on the TV. I sat through the news, but Stacey's helicopter wasn't mentioned once.

Breakfast wasn't exactly a laff riot, needless to say. I felt kind of relieved when Mr. Reynolds picked me up in the lobby.

How was the job? Just fine. The kids were easy. The parents didn't mind if they ate junk food. We spent most of the day outdoors. What more could you ask for?

After lunch, Scott and Lani went off to play in the den and I put Raymond down for a nap. Mr. Reynolds's dad was due any minute. I was starting to think about Stacey a lot, and I was anxious to get back to the hotel.

As I walked back to the living room, I passed the Reynoldses' wall of family photos. Wall *and* table, that is.

Mary Anne had mentioned that the older Mr. Reynolds was Caucasian, and he kind of stood out in the pictures.

She didn't tell me he was in World War Two, though.

A letter of commendation from the president, a Flying Cross, a Purple Heart . . .

Gulp.

My own heart was turning purple.

This was a war hero. He fought against the Japanese. He lived in Hawaii, he married a Hawaiian woman.

And he was about to come here.

Did Mary Anne know this? She must have. This was sabotage.

Why had she done this to me?

I couldn't let him see me.

I could hold a newspaper in front of my face. Make a paper bag mask and tell him the kids forced me to keep it on.

Ding-dong! "Anybody home?"

I couldn't move. My feet had become one with the carpet.

"Grandpaaaaa!" Lani and Scott screamed as they ran for him.

I eyed the back door.

"Hiiii!" answered the elder Mr. Reynolds. "So, where's the young lady from Connecticut?"

He was stepping closer. In a moment he would leave the front vestibule and face me.

Thank goodness no guns were mounted on the walls.

"There you are," he said, looming into view.

We were eye-to-eye. All I could think to say was "I'm sorry." My brain ordered up the words, but my mouth refused to move. It just hung open.

"Welcome to Hawaii. I'm Sam Reynolds." Mr. Reynolds held out his hand.

I checked it for weapons, then shook it. "C-C — " I cleared my parched throat. "Claudia Kishi."

"Grandpa has medals," Lani reported.

"He was a war hero," Scott said. "Pow-pow-pow!"

The sound effects were not helping my mood one bit.

"Well, I lived through it." Mr. Reynolds chuckled. "I guess that's heroic enough. Have a seat, Claudia. Can I get you a soda? I think I'll have one."

"Okay."

Mr. Reynolds disappeared into the kitchen.

I was numb. He couldn't have missed who I was. What I represented. Yet he hadn't flinched a bit. He was just as nice as can be.

Maybe his eyes were bad.

He returned to the living room, gave me a can of soda, and sank into an armchair with a big smile. I could hear Scott and Lani playing in the den.

"Tell me, Claudia, have you seen the sights?" he asked. "Honolulu, Waikiki, Pearl Harbor . . ."

"Yeah, all of those."

"Want to move here yet? Everybody does. I sure did, first time I laid eyes on this place."

"Was that . . . during the war?" I asked.

Mr. Reynolds took a sip of his soda. "You bet. I was involved in the clean-up at Pearl Harbor."

"And . . . well, you don't . . . when you see . . . you don't mind . . ."

Mr. Reynolds smiled. "Pardon me?"

I inhaled deeply. "Well, to be honest, I hated visiting Pearl Harbor, Mr. Reynolds."

He looked puzzled. "Why's that?"

The words just flew out. "All those bombs. All those wasted lives. On a Sunday morning, when no one expected it. I mean, how can anyone ever forget that, or forgive it? It — it just made me feel so ashamed. You know, to be Japanese."

There. I'd said it. I'd finally gotten it off my chest. To a survivor of the disaster.

Mr. Reynolds didn't say anything for a moment. He didn't look angry, just thoughtful.

"In my family," he finally said, "legend has it that my Scottish great-great-great-grandfather, Duncan Reynolds, burned another man's farm. Killed all his animals and injured his son, all in a feud over money. Well, he was run out of town for that. He became penniless and sank into a life of terrible, heartless crime. Black-Hearted Duncan, they called him. The legend still survives."

"How awful."

"And you know what? When I go back to that same town, I'm treated like a hero. Sure, they tease me about it, but I've stayed friendly with one of the descendants of the man whose farm was burned."

"He doesn't mind?"

"They were different people, those ancestors. We can't be held responsible for them. Even in a case like mine, in which it's a direct descendant. Do you know where your ancestors stood during the war?"

"No . . ."

"Well, you can't take on the burden of an entire country, can you? And frankly, no one has the right to put that burden on you, either."

You know what popped into my mind? The way the U.S. government had herded away Japanese-Americans to detention camps. A big burden sure was put on them.

"Besides, Claudia," Mr. Reynolds said, "the atom bombs made Pearl Harbor look small by comparison."

Mr. Reynolds looked straight ahead for a few moments. He and I were both lost in thought.

Finally he took a swig of his soda. "Anyhow, that's one reason I like Hawaii. People tolerate and respect each other pretty well here. I guess that's all we can do, isn't it?"

"Grandpaaaa!" Lani wailed, running into the living room. "Scott said I had armpit breath!"

Mr. Reynolds raised an eyebrow. "Of course, our tolerance does have limits," he said out of the corner of his mouth.

Boy, did I feel better. It seemed as if a huge sack had been lifted from my shoulders.

Well, sort of. Another sack was underneath.

I began thinking about Stacey again.

When Mr. Reynolds (the Younger) arrived to take me back to the hotel, his face was grim.

"Any news about my friend?" I asked.

"Your teacher was on the phone when I left," he said. "I didn't have time to find out what happened."

I said quick good-byes and ran out to the car.

Mr. Reynolds sped back to the hotel. As we pulled into the hotel driveway, my heart was fluttering.

I could see a throng of kids in the lobby. Everyone was talking. They must have heard something.

CHAPTER 20

Dawn

Monday

Mallory, as I write this, at 9:30 A.M., Hawaii time, Stacey has not been found. Everyone is on tenterhooks. I'm not exactly sure what tenterhooks are, but we're on them. You'd know what I mean if you were here.

I simply can't stand to wait around the hotel. If I do I'll just explode.

Ms. Bernhardt agreed to take a long walk with me. I have a project I've been meaning to do, and now seems like the perfect time.

I'll need help, though. Maybe I can twist a few arms....

"What do you mean, go to a beach?" Abby asked. "How can you think of a beach at a time like this?"

"I mean, *the* beach," I replied. "The one Jessi and I went to yesterday."

"The garbage dump?" Jessi said. "Dawn, you're weird."

"Look," I pressed on, "I talked to Mrs. Reynolds about this. She thinks it's a great idea. She agreed to give me these huge biodegradable garbage bags. It won't take long, and Ms. Bernhardt says she'll go with us. We can't do much good moping around here."

Mary Anne had already refused to go. She was sobbing softly on a sofa nearby, and Logan was trying to cheer her up. It was the closest I'd seen them on the whole trip.

"So we're going to clean up a beach?" Abby asked. "How . . . ecologically correct."

"I hate that phrase," I said.

"All right, all right, I'll go," Abby said.

"Mrs. Reynolds is going to meet us at the side entrance with the bags," I said. "You coming, Jessi?"

She sighed. "I guess."

We went upstairs to get Ms. Bernhardt from her room. On the way down we checked at the front desk for news of Stacey (nothing yet). Then we went outside and picked up the bags.

Ms. Bernhardt carried them as we walked toward the water. Once again, as we approached the ridge, kids' voices rang out. We climbed to the top and gazed over.

Abby made a face. "Ew. We're supposed to clean *this*?"

"Honey, we're going to need a bulldozer," Ms. Bernhardt remarked.

"No, we're not." I took one of the bags from her and walked down to the beach. I picked up the first piece of litter I saw, an old bike tire, and threw it in.

"What are you doing?"

I turned to see a boy and a girl, about ten years old, running toward me.

"Picking up trash," I said.

"Are you the janitor?" asked the girl.

"Nope, just a visitor," I replied. "But I think this beach looks kind of gross, don't you?"

"Yukio! Jeanette! Come here!" the boy called.

A younger boy and girl rushed over.

I continued stuffing garbage into my bag. Jessi called out, "I'll start at the other end."

"I've got the *mauka* side!" Abby exclaimed, running to the back of the beach.

"Trash detail in Hawaii," Ms. Bernhardt mumbled. "Who'd have ever thought?"

Before long, the kids were grabbing bags and helping out. The older boy and girl were

187

d Danny and Pohaikealoha (Pohai, for
). Yukio and Jeanette were their friends.
by held up a ripped, seaweed-encrusted
ing shoe. "Hmmm, what shoe size are
u, Dawn?"

"Very funny," I said.

"My goodness!" Ms. Bernhardt exclaimed,
picking up a discarded bathing suit. "This person must have had a chilly trip home."

The kids cracked up at that.

We found all kinds of interesting things on
the sand and in the water — a chicken skeleton,
a few clumps of dog hair, a Grateful Dead cassette, a steering wheel, a California Angels
baseball cap, and a stethoscope (don't ask me).

Jessi was like a trash magnet. She filled three
bags right away.

The kids? Well, let's just say they weren't
as efficient, but they had the most energy.

"I have nine things in my bag!" Yukio
announced.

"I have thirteen!" Jeanette said.

"That's because yours are smaller."

"So?"

Pohai stepped between them. "Hey, we're
a team," she said. "It's us against the trash."

"Yeah, what's our name?" Yukio asked.

"Um . . . the Anti-Litter Bugs," Pohai replied.

"Yyyyes!" Yukio pumped his fist into the air.

Pohai was definitely the Kristy Thomas of

up. I smiled at her and said, "I guess
the Head Bug."

ai smiled back. "I'm the oldest."

know that expression, "Many hands
light work"? Well, it sure was true that
ay. In about an hour we'd hauled all the
garbage to the Dumpster.

Afterward we stood on the ridge, tired but
thrilled.

"Wow, it's actually pretty," Abby said.

It was, too. A perfect little crescent of sand
with a gentle surf.

"I want it to stay like this forever," Pohai
remarked.

"It can." I nodded toward the pile of bags that
remained. "Those are yours. Hand one out to
everyone who comes to the beach from now on."

"What happens when we run out?" Pohai asked.

"Buy more, silly," Yukio said.

"We could put out trash cans, too," Danny
suggested.

"And a sign that says 'Do Not Litter,' "
Jeanette added.

"But we'd have to buy them," Danny explained. "That's expensive."

"Well, how could you and your friends raise
money?" I asked.

"Oooh! Oooh!" Jeanette raised her hand, as
if she were in class. "In school we had a bake
sale to raise money."

"What about a walkathon?" Jessi asked. "Sign up people to pledge an amount for every mile you walk."

"Or a readathon," Abby said. "Same idea, but it's money for every book you read, or every page you read."

"Five dollars a page," Danny said excitedly. "And I'll read *Mossflower*."

"Well, something like that," I said.

"Can we swim now?" Jeanette whined.

"Last one in is a rotten banana!" Pohai shouted.

As they raced to the water, screaming, I shouted a good-bye.

"I'm impressed," Ms. Bernhardt said. "Do you think you could do something about the faculty lounge when we go home, Dawn? It's turned into such a pigsty."

Walking back to the hotel, I felt pretty good. I know it sounds corny, but I really believe that if we each clean up a little corner of this world, it'll be a better place to live in. I hoped Pohai and her friends would stay committed.

Mary Anne was pacing in front of the SeaView as we approached. When she saw us, she came running.

She was grinning from ear to ear.

"Guess what?" she shouted. "They found Stacey!"

CHAPTER 21

Stacey

Monday

Well, Mal, I survived.

By the time you read this, you'll already know that. But you may not know the whole story. You may not know that our helicopter crash-landed. And that we were stranded overnight in the middle of a forest. And that Robert Brewster almost collapsed of a broken heart.

I WOULDN'T GO THAT FAR.

Okay, that was just a rumor. Anyway, let me tell you, I saw a part of Hawaii NO ONE ever sees...

W*hucka-whucka-whucka-whucka* . . .

We heard the rotor blades above us, but we couldn't see a helicopter.

Pete Black was waving frantically at the patch of blank blue sky between the treetops. *"Over here! Over here!"*

"He can't hear you!" Mr. Fredericks shouted. "Let's find a clearing!"

Mr. Fredericks raced away between the trees. Pete, Mari, Renee, and I followed close behind him. The tree cover was pretty thick, and sunlight broke through only in small patches.

By the time we reached a clearing, the chopper was gone.

We all sank to the ground, breathless.

"They'll come back," Mr. Fredericks assured us.

"What if they don't?" Renee asked.

Mr. Fredericks looked straight up. "Okay, the sun is setting to our right. I know we went down in the Kahikinui Forest Reserve. That means if we walk away from the sun, to the east, we should hit the western ridge of the Kaupō Gap. We follow that south, to the right, and we'll reach the town of Kaupō. Got that?"

"Uh, we'll just follow you," Pete said.

"How long is it?" Mari asked.

"As the crow flies, nine or ten miles," Mr. Fredericks replied.

"How about as the feet walk?" I asked.

"Maybe fifteen."

Fifteen miles? I looked down at my lightweight aerobics shoes.

I felt very sorry for my feet.

And for me.

As everyone began walking, I glanced at my watch. It was already three o'clock, and I'd missed my lunch. "Mr. Fredericks, I have to eat," I called out. "I'm a diabetic. I have a supply of emergency food and insulin in my pack, but only enough for a day or so."

"Hold up!" Mr. Fredericks yelled ahead. "Take your time, Stacey. And don't worry, you'll be sitting in a hotel twenty-four hours from now. Trust me."

I quickly took off my pack and tried as hard as I could to believe him.

Now, I was born and raised in New York City. For me, a nature walk meant a stroll around the Central Park reservoir.

That was not terrific preparation for a fifteen-mile hike through volcanic forest. I kept stepping on rocks and roots. If I wasn't twisting my ankle, I was bruising my instep.

Pete, Mari, and Renee, however, were not from NYC. I was discovering that they were not fully human at all. They were, in fact, part mountain goat. They were scampering ahead, yakking away, having a delightful time.

Me? I groped along, clutching onto vines for support, moaning, feeling my blisters grow like the Bubble Cave of Haleakalā.

Soon the sun was casting long, creepy shadows. We rested near a spot that looked exactly like the one we'd started from.

"Are we any closer?" I asked.

"Can't you smell the saltwater?" Mr. Fredericks asked.

We all sniffed. We all shook our heads.

I took my shoes off. My ankles rejoiced. My toes were singing hallelujah. "I don't know if I can make it," I said.

"It's too dark to go on, anyway," Mr. Fredericks said. "We'll camp here. We can pool whatever food and water we have, get some sleep, then start again in the morning."

Walk again? I couldn't imagine it.

Wearily I found a secluded area where I could give myself an insulin injection and not gross out Pukey Pete. Then I went back to the group. Fortunately, Renee and Mari had brought along juice boxes and trail gorp. We ate and drank a somber meal. Then I found a comfortable spot and fell into a deep sleep. As I dozed off, I could hear Pete and Mari talking worriedly while Mr. Fredericks paced back and forth.

The next morning is a haze in my memory. I recall the screaming pain in my feet. I recall not eating enough breakfast, and being on the verge of unconsciousness.

And I remember reaching a dirt road, where a red Land Rover bounced by and stopped to give us a lift.

I must have passed out, because when I awoke, I was in a hospital room, hooked up to an IV tube. It took my eyes awhile to focus on the person standing over my bed.

"Hi, Stacey."

I blinked a few times. I had to be dreaming. "Robert?"

When he smiled, I realized I was awake. Because dreams never cause real tears to roll down my cheeks.

"The helicopter company flew us here," he said.

"Where is this place? How did I get here?"

"Hana. Your whole group was picked up by a local guy. He drove you here. It's a good thing, too. The doctors said your blood sugar was dangerously low."

Behind Robert, I could see the others — Pete, Mari, Renee, Mr. Fredericks, Mr. De Young, and the kids from the other helicopter. They were all smiling, except for Pete, who looked totally grossed out by the mushy scene.

Well, I didn't care. I threw my arms around Robert and hugged him as hard as I could.

Fortunately, I wasn't bedridden very long. When my blood sugar stabilized, the doctors let me go.

I held Robert's hand as we left the hospital. I sat with him on the bus ride back to Kahului (no, I did not want to take the helicopter).

I did have to ride in a plane, though, because Mr. De Young had scheduled a flight back to Honolulu. I sat with Robert on that, too.

He was being so nice to me. Bea Foster, who was in the other helicopter group, said he'd been crying all day. (Robert denied that, of course. But I believe it.)

Snuggling against him in that plane, I felt comfortable and warm. I hadn't felt that way with him in a long time.

"Robert, I'm really sorry I was such a pill," I said.

Robert shrugged. "I'm sorry I was ignoring you."

"And I'm sorry I sat behind you!" Pete Black groaned from the seat in back of us.

We both burst out laughing.

As our plane began to descend toward the airport, Robert whispered in my ear, "I *was* crying. I thought we'd lost you."

I smiled and gave him a kiss.

I could hear Pete scrambling for the barf bag.

Once we landed in Honolulu, Mr. De Young rented yet another minivan, and we drove up the coast to the North Shore of Oahu. We pulled up in front of a group of cottages.

Jessi's face appeared in a window. I could hear her scream through the glass. Moments later, the entire BSC was racing toward us.

My feet were still killing me. Robert had to prop me up after I climbed out of the minivan.

Did Claudia care about my fragile condition? Did Mary Anne, or Dawn, or Abby, or Jessi? Not at all.

They mobbed me. They screamed in my face. They picked me up. They hugged me. They dripped their tears all over my blouse.

And you know what? I didn't feel any pain at all.

Not a bit.

CHAPTER 22

Jessi

Tuesday

Stacey's back! And she's okay, except for a sunburned neck and blistered feet. She told us her story while we all sat on the beach and watched the surfers.

Guess what? Last night when we went to the Polynesian Cultural Center, Robert pushed Stacey around in a rented wheelchair!

But first things first. Back to Jessi's Guided Tour. Okay.

Oahu's North Shore. We started in Haleiwa, which means "Home of the Frigate Bird." Very quaint. Then, after Stacey arrived, we visited the most famous surfing beaches in the world....

"Calm?" I said. "This is calm?"

We were standing on Sunset Beach. The waves were rising up like enormous sea monster jaws, then crashing to the shore. A few surfers and Boogie boarders were out that day, and some people were even body-surfing.

I thought they were crazy.

"These are only ten-footers," Dawn the Surfer explained. "Summer is the off-season. In winter the waves are huge. That's when the championships are held."

As a wave came in, I held up my cassette recorder and said into the mike, "Mallory, this is the sound of a small wave on the North Shore of Oahu."

BOOOOOOM!
Very dramatic.

Stacey was sitting on a lounge chair we'd brought from our cottage. Surrounded by SMS kids, she was telling the story of her crash and rescue for about the twentieth time. By now the story was, well, growing.

" . . . The other helicopter passed so close we could smell the exhaust," she was saying. "We looked around for dry kindling for smoke signals. All we saw were strange footprints leading into a cave . . ."

I tried to tape-record her, but Stacey wouldn't let me. She said she'd write about it in the journal.

I, of course, wrote a lot, especially during our evening trip:

We're now at this huge place called the Polynesian Cultural Center. It's kind of a theme park, only better. You walk through authentic re-creations of ancient tribal villages. People in costumes invite you to join in as they perform rituals, dance, and play music. Mary Anne made cloth out of tree bark. Dawn pounded taro root into poi. I danced the hula in a Tahiti exhibit, complete with grass skirt. (You should have heard Alan Gray laughing. I wanted to strangle him.)

Just past the Fiji display, a woman sidled up to Stacey's wheelchair. "You're the girl on the news, aren't you?" she asked. "The helicopter crash?"

"Uh . . . yeah." Stacey looked around nervously, as if she were expecting a practical joke.

Well, you would not believe the crowd that gathered. About twenty people wanted to shake Stacey's hand. They'd all seen her story on the TV news. Some of them followed us all the way to the *luau* at the center's restaurant.

Do you know the main feature of a *luau*? A roasted pig. (Dawn threatened to boycott it, but instead she stuck to the vegetarian buffet.) After that we saw a huge, splashy revue called "Mana!" complete with an exploding volcano. That was cool.

I took notes for Mallory during the activities. I took notes during the show. I took so many notes I had to start a new spiral notebook. I also took a whole roll of photos, my thirteenth.

That night, Abby, Claudia, Dawn, Mary Anne, Logan, Stacey, Robert, and I all stayed up late gabbing. After we reminisced about Honolulu and Windward Oahu, Logan turned to Stacey and asked what she'd been afraid of most in her jungle adventure.

"Well," Stacey replied as we all leaned in, "the one-eyed hermit was definitely pretty horrible, but the Great Haleakalā Lava Beast was the worst."

We were howling until midnight.

By the next morning, Stacey was walking again. To celebrate, Mr. De Young took a group of us to Haleiwa, where Stacey bought new sneakers.

They came in handy on our hike in Waimea Falls Park. A new set of fingers would have helped me a lot. Mine were aching from so much journal writing. I abbreviated that day:

Fed peacocks and guinea fowl. Almost had finger bitten off by goose. Saw amazing flowers, wood-carvers, hula demonstrations. Watched guy jump off fifty-five-foot rock.

Don't worry, the guy in that last part was a professional diver, who plunged into the water at the base of the falls. (My heart nearly leaped into the water with him.)

Around noon it was beach time again. A lot of kids swam, but not me. I went off with Mary Anne to explore tidal pools.

When we came back, Dawn was giving Logan a surfing lesson.

Sort of. Actually, it was more like a standing

lesson. Poor Logan. He's great on the football field, but on the board? Forget it. He spent most of his time underwater.

"Lo-GAN! Lo-GAN! Lo-GAN!" people were cheering.

Alan and Pete were strumming air guitars and wailing out their own version of a Beach Boys song: "Everybody's gone suuuuurfin', over Logan's head . . ."

Well, Logan survived (and Alan's lesson was even worse). Our post-surf lunch was at Matsumoto, where we all had "shaved ice," a fancy kind of snow cone. Mine was covered with pineapple, banana, and mango syrups. Dawn's was filled with . . . azuki beans. (Yes, I'm serious. Dawn would have put brussels sprouts in her cone if they had been offered.)

Then off to a banana plantation. An airplane stunt show. A climb to a temple where the ancient Hawaiians made ritual human sacrifices to the gods (for some reason, we all looked at Alan Gray).

What a day. At the end of it I wrote this:

Dinner at a roadside restaurant. Stacey told latest version of rescue tale, something about skydivers and vine-swinging over molten lava. Abby promised to tell Stacey's adventure to "Steve." (Spielberg, that is. She's convinced he's going to call.)

What a great, GREAT day this was! Especially now that we're all together. I can't believe tomorrow we'll be home.

I almost feel that the trip should be starting now, not ending. Stacey and Robert look happy together. Claudia's not brooding. Dawn has seven islands full of beachfront she can clean.

Mary Anne and Logan still aren't doing stuff together, but you can tell they want to. And I have half a spiral notebook left.

Don't worry, Mal. I miss home. I can't wait to see you. But I really feel attached to Hawaii now.

I think part of me will always feel that way.

CHAPTER 23

LOGAN

WEDNESDAY

HI, MAL. I'M WRITING IN THIS
THING, TOO. MIGHT AS WELL. THIS
IS GOING TO BE A LONG FLIGHT
AND I'M ALREADY RUNNING OUT OF
STUFF TO DO.

AND AFTER THIS WE HAVE ANOTHER
FIVE-HOUR FLIGHT! I DON'T KNOW
WHAT I'LL DO ON THAT ONE. MAYBE
JUST TALK TO MARY ANNE.

SHE JUST PUNCHED ME IN THE
SHOULDER. I DON'T KNOW WHY.
I TAKE SUCH ABUSE!

DID JESSI TELL YOU ABOUT MY
SURFING LESSON? DON'T BELIEVE
HER. I WAS A REAL POUND MASTER...

That was an expression I learned. It means "a great surfer."

Mary Anne thought it meant someone who took a real pounding. She says that definition fits better.

No one wants to admit the truth. I, Logan Bruno, caught a wave. Okay, not a big one. But I traveled forward, and that counts.

If I'd had a second chance, I'd be ready for the Banzai Pipeline.

Unfortunately, on Wednesday we had to fly home.

We packed, scarfed down breakfast, and piled into the minivans we'd been using all week. Of course, Mary Anne and I were in different ones.

Which I thought was pretty dumb.

See, we'd had this experiment, TBI. Together But Independent. Mainly it was to make our friends happy. They had been saying Mary Anne and I were like Siamese twins.

It was cool. It had worked okay. But enough was enough.

Not that I was pining away for Mary Anne or anything. I just felt funny. If I wanted to talk to her, joke around or something, even comfort her about Stacey, I thought I couldn't. Like I was breaking the rules.

Okay, I kind of missed her. I admit it.

So I sat with her in the terminal as we waited for the flight. "What seat do you have?" I asked.

Mary Anne checked her ticket. "Twenty-two L."

"I have fifteen A," I said with a sigh. "Oh, well, at least I get a window."

"Twenty-three L!" Claudia called out.

"Ten C!" Mari Drabek piped up.

"Twenty-two K!" said Alan Gray.

"Bingo!" shouted Pete Black.

Everyone started laughing. Except Mary Anne. Her face was ghostly white.

Mine would be, too, if I had to sit next to Alan Gray.

I had an idea. "Hey, Alan," I called out, "want a window seat?"

"You bet I do, surfer dude. What's up, afraid of heights?"

What a dork. I wanted to slam him.

Oh, well, sometimes you just have to put up and shut up. At least I had my seat next to Mary Anne.

"Thanks, Logan," Mary Anne said.

The boarding announcement blared over the speakers. Everybody stood up and scrambled for the door.

Ms. Bernhardt and Mr. Wong were already there, and guess what they were holding?

Two boxes of real Hawaiian *leis*!

"We didn't get 'em when we came in," Ms. Bernhardt said. "So we'll get 'em going out!"

Yyyyyes! That's what I call a teacher.

The plane smelled like a flower shop when we walked in. Mary Anne and I settled into our seats for the long ride.

How long? Take-off was 7:05, then five hours to L.A., an hour layover, five hours to N.Y.C., and a two-hour bus ride to Stoneybrook.

No one seemed to mind too much. As the plane took off, Claudia and Abby began reviewing the whole ten days, minute by minute, in the seats behind us. Dawn and Jessi were already writing postcards to some kids they'd met at a beach. Robert and Stacey were whispering to each other.

"I'm glad we're sitting together, Logan," Mary Anne said.

"Me, too." I smiled.

Together we watched the Hawaiian Islands shrink away to the size of little pebbles.

"You know, I have a secret," Mary Anne said softly.

"What?" I asked.

"I hated TBI."

"So did I."

"Really?"

"Really."

"Why didn't you say so?"

213

"Why didn't you?"

We looked at each other. Then we both cracked up.

"Well, at least our friends aren't complaining anymore," Mary Anne pointed out. "We spent lots of time with them."

"Too much time," I said. "If I have to look in Trevor's and Austin's ugly faces one more time, I think I'll die."

Spitballs came flying at me from both sides. Mary Anne and I ducked.

It was true, though. Never again would I let my friends tell me how much time to spend with my girlfriend. I mean, what was the point? I'd just spent ten days in Hawaii avoiding the person I wanted to be with most.

"Next trip," Mary Anne whispered, "no TBI."

I nodded. "I hear the social studies classes are visiting the Stoneybrook Dump in September."

"Save me a seat," Mary Anne said with a big grin.

By the time we arrived in hot, muggy New York City, I felt as if I'd been run over by a truck. I was sweaty and tired, and my *lei* was starting to smell like seaweed. It was eleven at night, and we still had a two-hour bus ride to Stoneybrook ahead of us.

Shuffling through Kennedy Airport with our wilted *leis*, we looked like the Death Marchers of ancient Oahu.

Tempers were short at the luggage pick-up area. Mr. De Young yelled at Austin. Mari yelled at Pete. Abby yelled at whoever happened to be near. Everyone yelled at Alan.

Me? I wasn't angry at anybody.

Neither was Mary Anne.

We quietly retrieved our luggage and found seats together on the bus. As we drove away, watching the lights of the New York City skyline, we slowly drifted off to sleep.

I know it sounds weird, but that was one of my favorite parts of the trip.

EPILOGUE

We arrived in Stoneybrook around 1:45 A.M. The weather was hot and muggy. My dad had to carry me to the car.

And that's the end.

Whew.

Mal, this was fun. I hope you enjoy reading it as much as I enjoyed writing it.

And taking the pictures.

And making the tape.

Next time, though, I'm bringing a secretary.

Remember my "typical Hawaiian family," the Reynoldses? Guess whose voice was on Claudia's answering machine when she arrived home?

Scott's. He had copied down the number on my T-shirt. Then he asked his grandfather for the Connecticut area code. He wanted to know if Claudia or I could baby-sit next week.

I'm going to have to call him back.

Kristy's going to be in Hawaii then. You think we should ask her?

Mal, if you ever go to Hawaii, take lots of sunscreen. And not the Day-Nite brand, either. It stinks. My skin is coming off in chunks. I look like something from the X-Files. Aha! Maybe thats my next career move.

I told my parints about my big Perl Harber dilemna. They didnt' lauhg at me atall. Dad said his older cusin was injurred fiting for the U.S. A Japanese-American freind of his spent his childhood in an inturnmint camp. Dad says its normul to hav complicated feelings about World War 2.

You now what mom told me? mimi never mentioned a word about the war. She refusd to talk about it.

Oh well I gess there are somethings youll never kno, huh?

I am so glad I went on this trip. My friends back home are going to be so jealous.
Maybe I can go back to Hawaii someday. I'm sure it's cheaper from the West Coast.

I'm dying to revisit my little beach and see if the kids are keeping it clean.

Which brings me to a new topic. I've noticed the condition of Brenner Field has really deteriorated since I moved away. I think this should be the first order of business on Wednesday....

Mom burst into tears when she saw me. Dad was with her, too. He'd driven all the way from NYC. They knew I was fine. They just wanted to see with their own eyes, I guess.

We stayed up all night. I showed them my blisters. I went over every little detail of my accident at least twice.

Well, almost every one. I left out the fire-breathing chimpanzees. I didn't think they could handle that.

Afterword

Hi, Mallory. I hope you like this journal. I think we covered everything. I'm sure you're going to hear it all over and over again in person.

Oh, well, if we repeat ourselves too much, just bop us over the head, okay?

With love to my best friend in the world,
Jessi

Dear Jessi,

This note is to say thank you thank you thank you thank you thank you thank you! (I wanted to write it a million times, but I thought Dawn would yell at me for wasting paper.)

Don't worry, I won't bop anyone. You can repeat all those stories as many times as you want.

Tell my parents, too. I'm working on them for a trip next year.

Leave out the helicopter crash, though, okay?

Thanks again, Jess. I will treasure this the rest of my life.

Love,
Mallory

P.S. Can you stand by to baby-sit for me on Saturday? I booked the job while you guys were away, but I'm having second thoughts. The family's name is Wellfleet, and I'll tell you all about them at the next meeting.

L. GODWIN

Ann M. Martin

About the Author

ANN MATTHEWS MARTIN was born on August 12, 1955. She grew up in Princeton, NJ, with her parents and her younger sister, Jane.

Although Ann used to be a teacher and then an editor of children's books, she's now a full-time writer. She gets the ideas for her books from many different places. Some are based on personal experiences. Others are based on childhood memories and feelings. Many are written about contemporary problems or events.

All of Ann's characters, even the members of the Baby-sitters Club, are made up. (So is Stoneybrook.) But many of her characters are based on real people. Sometimes Ann names her characters after people she knows, other times she chooses names she likes.

In addition to the Baby-sitters Club books, Ann Martin has written many other books for children. Her favorite is *Ten Kids, No Pets* because she loves big families and she loves animals. Her favorite Baby-sitters Club book is *Kristy's Big Day*. (By the way, Kristy is her favorite baby-sitter!)

Ann M. Martin now lives in New York with her cats, Gussie and Woody. Her hobbies are reading, sewing, and needlework — especially making clothes for children.

THE BABY-SITTERS CLUB®

The best friends you'll ever have!

Collect 'em all!

by Ann M. Martin

More titles...

The Baby-sitters Club titles continued...

☐ MG48222-X	#78	Claudia and the Crazy Peaches	$3.50
☐ MG48223-8	#79	Mary Anne Breaks the Rules	$3.50
☐ MG48224-6	#80	Mallory Pike, #1 Fan	$3.50
☐ MG48225-4	#81	Kristy and Mr. Mom	$3.50
☐ MG48226-2	#82	Jessi and the Troublemaker	$3.50
☐ MG48235-1	#83	Stacey vs. the BSC	$3.50
☐ MG48228-9	#84	Dawn and the School Spirit War	$3.50
☐ MG48236-X	#85	Claudi Kishli, Live from WSTO	$3.50
☐ MG48227-0	#86	Mary Anne and Camp BSC	$3.50
☐ MG48237-8	#87	Stacey and the Bad Girls	$3.50
☐ MG22872-2	#88	Farewell, Dawn	$3.50
☐ MG22873-0	#89	Kristy and the Dirty Diapers	$3.50
☐ MG22874-9	#90	Welcome to the BSC, Abby	$3.50
☐ MG22875-1	#91	Claudia and the First Thanksgiving	$3.50
☐ MG22876-5	#92	Mallory's Christmas Wish	$3.50
☐ MG22877-3	#93	Mary Anne and the Memory Garden	$3.99
☐ MG22878-1	#94	Stacey McGill, Super Sitter	$3.99
☐ MG45575-3		Logan's Story Special Edition Readers' Request	$3.25
☐ MG47118-X		Logan Bruno, Boy Baby-sitter Special Edition Readers' Request	$3.50
☐ MG47756-0		Shannon's Story Special Edition	$3.50
☐ MG47686-6		The Baby-sitters Club Guide to Baby-sitting	$3.25
☐ MG47314-X		The Baby-sitters Club Trivia and Puzzle Fun Book	$2.50
☐ MG48400-1		BSC Portrait Collection: Claudia's Book	$3.50
☐ MG22864-1		BSC Portrait Collection: Dawn's Book	$3.50
☐ MG48399-4		BSC Portrait Collection: Stacey's Book	$3.50
☐ MG47151-1		The Baby-sitters Club Chain Letter	$14.95
☐ MG48295-5		The Baby-sitters Club Secret Santa	$14.95
☐ MG45074-3		The Baby-sitters Club Notebook	$2.50
☐ MG44783-1		The Baby-sitters Club Postcard Book	$4.95

Available wherever you buy books...or use this order form.

Scholastic Inc., P.O. Box 7502, 2931 E. McCarty Street, Jefferson City, MO 65102

Please send me the books I have checked above. I am enclosing $_____ (please add $2.00 to cover shipping and handling). Send check or money order–no cash or C.O.D.s please.

Name _____ Birthdate_____

Address _____

City_____ State/Zip _____

Please allow four to six weeks for delivery. Offer good in the U.S. only. Sorry, mail orders are not available to residents of Canada. Prices subject to change.

THE BABY-SITTERS CLUB®

by Ann M. Martin

Collect and read these exciting BSC Super Specials, Mysteries, and Super Mysteries along with your favorite Baby-sitters Club books!

BSC Super Specials

❏ BBK44240-6	Baby-sitters on Board! Super Special #1	$3.95
❏ BBK44239-2	Baby-sitters' Summer Vacation Super Special #2	$3.95
❏ BBK43973-1	Baby-sitters' Winter Vacation Super Special #3	$3.95
❏ BBK42493-9	Baby-sitters' Island Adventure Super Special #4	$3.95
❏ BBK43575-2	California Girls! Super Special #5	$3.95
❏ BBK43576-0	New York, New York! Super Special #6	$3.95
❏ BBK44963-X	Snowbound! Super Special #7	$3.95
❏ BBK44962-X	Baby-sitters at Shadow Lake Super Special #8	$3.95
❏ BBK45661-X	Starring The Baby-sitters Club! Super Special #9	$3.95
❏ BBK45674-1	Sea City, Here We Come! Super Special #10	$3.95
❏ BBK47015-9	The Baby-sitters Remember Super Special #11	$3.95
❏ BBK48308-0	Here Come the Bridesmaids! Super Special #12	$3.95

BSC Mysteries

❏ BAI44084-5	#1 Stacey and the Missing Ring	$3.50
❏ BAI44085-3	#2 Beware Dawn!	$3.50
❏ BAI44799-8	#3 Mallory and the Ghost Cat	$3.50
❏ BAI44800-5	#4 Kristy and the Missing Child	$3.50
❏ BAI44801-3	#5 Mary Anne and the Secret in the Attic	$3.50
❏ BAI44961-3	#6 The Mystery at Claudia's House	$3.50
❏ BAI44960-5	#7 Dawn and the Disappearing Dogs	$3.50
❏ BAI44959-1	#8 Jessi and the Jewel Thieves	$3.50
❏ BAI44958-3	#9 Kristy and the Haunted Mansion	$3.50

More titles ➡

The Baby-sitters Club books continued...

❏ BAI45696-2	#10 Stacey and the Mystery Money	$3.50
❏ BAI47049-3	#11 Claudia and the Mystery at the Museum	$3.50
❏ BAI47050-7	#12 Dawn and the Surfer Ghost	$3.50
❏ BAI47051-5	#13 Mary Anne and the Library Mystery	$3.50
❏ BAI47052-3	#14 Stacey and the Mystery at the Mall	$3.50
❏ BAI47053-1	#15 Kristy and the Vampires	$3.50
❏ BAI47054-X	#16 Claudia and the Clue in the Photograph	$3.50
❏ BAI48232-7	#17 Dawn and the Halloween Mystery	$3.50
❏ BAI48233-5	#18 Stacey and the Mystery at the Empty House	$3.50
❏ BAI48234-3	#19 Kristy and the Missing Fortune	$3.50
❏ BAI48309-9	#20 Mary Anne and the Zoo Mystery	$3.50
❏ BAI48310-2	#21 Claudia and the Recipe for Danger	$3.50
❏ BAI22866-8	#22 Stacey and the Haunted Masquerade	$3.50
❏ BAI22867-6	#23 Abby and the Secret Society	$3.99

BSC Super Mysteries

❏ BAI48311-0	The Baby-sitters' Haunted House Super Mystery #1	$3.99
❏ BAI22871-4	Baby-sitters Beware Super Mystery #2	$3.99

Available wherever you buy books...or use this order form.

Scholastic Inc., P.O. Box 7502, 2931 East McCarty Street, Jefferson City, MO 65102-7502

Please send me the books I have checked above. I am enclosing $ _____
(please add $2.00 to cover shipping and handling). Send check or money order
— no cash or C.O.D.s please.

Name_____Birthdate_____

Address _____

City_____State/Zip_____

Please allow four to six weeks for delivery. Offer good in the U.S. only. Sorry, mail orders are not
available to residents of Canada. Prices subject to change.

BSCM795

What's the scoop with Dawn, Kristy, Mallory, and the other girls?

Be the first to know with G★I★R★L★ magazine!

Hey, Baby-sitters Club readers! Now you can be the first on the block to get in on the action of G★I★R★L★ It's an exciting new magazine that lets you dig in and read...

★ Upcoming selections from Ann Martin's Baby-sitters Club books
★ Fun articles on handling stress, turning dreams into great careers, making and keeping best friends, and much more
★ Plus, all the latest on new movies, books, music, and sports!

To get in on the scoop, just cut and mail this coupon today. And don't forget to tell all your friends about G★I★R★L★ magazine!

A neat offer for you...6 issues for only $15.00.

Sign up today -- this special offer ends July 1, 1996!

❏ **YES!** Please send me G★I★R★L★ magazine. I will receive six fun-filled issues for only $15.00. Enclosed is a check (no cash, please) made payable to G★I★R★L★ for $15.00.

Just fill in, cut out, and mail this coupon with your payment of $15.00 to:
G★I★R★L★, c/o Scholastic Inc., 2931 East McCarty Street, Jefferson City, MO 65101.

Name _____

Address _____

City, State, ZIP _____

9013

Meet the best friends you'll ever have!

ALL NEW!

by Ann M. Martin

Have you heard? The BSC has a new look
—and more great stuff than ever before.
An all-new scrapbook for each book's narrator!
A letter from Ann M. Martin! Fill-in pages to
personalize your copy! Order today!

☐ BBD22473-5	#1	**Kristy's Great Idea**	$3.50
☐ BBD22763-7	#2	**Claudia and the Phantom Phone Calls**	$3.99
☐ BBD25158-9	#3	**The Truth About Stacey**	$3.99
☐ BBD25159-7	#4	**Mary Anne Saves the Day**	$3.50
☐ BBD25160-0	#5	**Dawn and the Impossible Three**	$3.50
☐ BBD25161-9	#6	**Kristy's Big Day**	$3.50
☐ BBD25162-7	#7	**Claudia and Mean Janine**	$3.50
☐ BBD25163-5	#8	**Boy Crazy Stacey**	$3.50
☐ BBD25164-3	#9	**The Ghost at Dawn's House**	$3.99
☐ BBD25165-1	#10	**Logan Likes Mary Anne!**	$3.99
☐ BBD25166-X	#11	**Kristy and the Snobs**	$3.99
☐ BBD25167-8	#12	**Claudia and the New Girl**	$3.99

Available wherever you buy books, or use this order form.